THE BAG-MAN VANISHES!

Docker was supposed to be OK . . . someone you could trust in a heroin deal.

All he had to do was hand over the money and get the stuff.

But he did more than that.

The courier was found dead, the chemist beaten . . . and everything gone.

And now the police and the whole San Francisco underworld were on his tail!

JOE GORES was a private investigator in San Francisco for a dozen years. He has written more than 100 short stories and four novels including the widely praised *Dead Skip* and *Final Notice* (both published by Ballantine).

Interface

by
Joe Gores

BALLANTINE BOOKS • NEW YORK

I wish to express my thanks to Doctor Joel Fort for invaluable technical assistance unselfishly given during the planning stages of this book.

JG

Library of Congress Catalog Card Number: 73-91882

SBN 345-24405-2-150

This edition published by arrangement with M. Evans and Company, Inc.

First Printing: March, 1976

Printed in the United States of America

BALLANTINE BOOKS
A Division of Random House, Inc.
201 East 50th Street, New York, N.Y. 10022
Simultaneously published by
Ballantine Books of Canada, Ltd., Toronto, Canada

For that Stark villain,
Parker—
because he's such
a beautiful human being

INTERFACE: the common boundary between two systems.

> We are creatures of a day.
> What is one, what is one not?
> Man is the dream of a shadow.
> Pindar's
> *Pythian* Odes

One

The dead Mexican lay on his back and stared at the ceiling. On the flat's close air still lingered the tang of gunpowder, but the unnatural angle of the Mexican's head suggested his Colt .38 had been a poor idea. He had gotten off one shot, then had been knocked backward over the sprung worn sofa, had landed on the back of his neck and had died.

The blond man flexed his hands once, like a wrestler who has thrown his opponent in the ring and is waiting for him to rise again.

"Goddam fool," he said aloud, even though he was quite alone in the shabby flat.

He looked like a wrestler, in fact, or a pro football player, apart from horn-rimmed glasses with dark heavy frames which gave his hard, bony face an unexpected scholar's cast. Ash-blond hair came nearly to his shoulders, and his short-sleeved white shirt, open at the throat, exposed arms which were lumped and knotted with muscle. His dark slacks emphasized the trimness of his waist and hips.

The blond man looked at his watch, looked at the dead Mexican, swore again, went to the window and drew aside the tattered lace curtains to peer out. He grunted at whatever he saw outside, and with sudden energy turned back from the window. When he moved there was a hesitation in his stride, a momentary check in the movement of his right leg almost too slight to be called a limp.

In the corner of the living room closest to the kitchen was the sort of Salvation Army dining table and chairs usually found in furnished flats in the Mission District.

1

On the table were a brown attaché case which looked very new, and a squatty, evil foot-high figure of brown clay which looked very ancient.

The blond man picked up the pottery figure. Seen up close it had mold marks down the sides, which made it much less than ancient but no less evil. He dropped it on the floor. It shattered. From the shards, the blond man picked up an ordinary Ziploc plastic bag. Inside the bag were a considerable number of much smaller sealed bags, also of clear plastic, which contained scant measures of white powder.

As he laid the Ziploc plastic bag on the table with gloved fingers, the doorbell echoed through the unheated and sparsely-furnished flat. The blond man padded down the hall, his steps slightly uneven on the bare wood floor, to push the old-fashioned iron door-opener. This disengaged the latch of the street door at the foot of the interior stairs.

"The front room," he called.

He turned away as the chemist started up, went back along the hall to the living room. He crossed the room to the attaché case and opened it. It was three-quarters filled with orderly rows of banded hundreds, not new. He dumped the Ziploc bag in on top of them, snapped shut the case again.

The chemist was old enough to have gotten only to the head of the stairs by that time, breathing heavily from the climb. He carried a black bag such as a doctor might carry, a small, precise man wearing a hat and an overcoat too heavy for the San Francisco autumn weather. Few San Franciscans wore a hat anymore. It, and the coat, made him look like someone mislaid during the twenties who was up and about again.

The chemist went up the hall. The hall was sufficiently dark to put the blond man in virtual silhouette at the end of it. His heavy shoulders, made sloping by the powerfully developed trapezius muscles, filled the living room doorway and blocked any chance view of the dead Mexican.

"You aren't Marquez," said the chemist, Addison, when he was close enough to be sure.

"I'm the bagman. This is my apartment."

The chemist stopped as if he had run into a turnstile.
"I only deal with Julio Marquez."

"Julio Marquez is dead."

"Dead?"

"I killed him," said the blond man.

As he spoke, he struck the chemist heavily in the face
with an almost casual swing of one club-like arm. The
chemist's hat flew off. His black bag slid several feet
down the hall with the sound of breaking glass as he
himself slid down the wall to a sitting position. His dam-
aged face looked like a cartoon face drawn to express
surprise.

The blond man checked the chemist's pulse, listened
to his respiration, loosened his tie, lifted an eyelid. He
was unconscious, his eyes rolled back, but he was
breathing steadily and his pulse was strong. The thread
of blood inching down out of his left nostril was too
slight to be from anything but tiny capillaries ruptured
by the force of the blow.

Leaving the chemist where he was, the blond man
went by him down the hall to the bathroom. The medicine chest held only two twenty-milligram ampules of
clear liquid. He looked at them thoughtfully.

"So it will work as well for the police as for the others," he said, again aloud.

One of the ampules slipped through his fingers to
shatter on the grey octagonal floor tiles below the wash-
basin. He left it there, replaced the other in the medicine
chest, went out without stepping into the mess.

In the front room he pulled on a black topcoat,
picked up the attaché case and started out without a
backward glance. Then he stopped. He stared at the
dead Mexican. He grinned. He squatted and opened the
attaché case. He opened the Ziploc bag, shoved the
dead hands, one after the other, down among the plastic
bags. The blond man left taking with him the dead
man's fingerprints, shut away in the attaché case.

The house was narrow, Victorian, painted grey and peeling, three-storied if you counted the ground floor which had no flat in it. The October morning was cold and bright, the sun just coming up and still without warmth. Two battered metal mailboxes were fixed to the door of the inset garage. The box for 1748 wore a new slip of paper with the word DOCKER typed on it.

The blond man, wearing his black topcoat and carrying his attaché case, appeared in the street door of 1748 through which the chemist had entered three or four minutes before. He descended the grey, chipped stairs to Bryant Street. The ornamentation of the black iron handrail was softened with a patina of old layered paint and was gritty with city dirt.

At the bottom of the stairs the blond man dropped the front door key into the mailbox for 1748. That made him the DOCKER typed on the slip of paper. He turned away, stripping off thin gloves of surgical rubber, pinching the attaché case between arm and body while his hands were busy. He looked both ways before stepping off the curb to cross deserted Bryant Street, ignoring the mustachioed youth sitting on a stoop a few doors away.

On the far side of the street was Franklin Square, which was bounded by Bryant, Potrero, Sixteenth and Seventeenth. Apart from this park and the nine houses on the even-numbered side of Bryant's 1700 block, it was a totally industrial area. To Docker's left was the site of the old Seals stadium, now a merchandise mart which itself had gone bankrupt in the midst of its mindless blacktop parking lots.

Docker tossed his attaché case up on the steep grass above the chest-high concrete retaining wall of the park, then jumped up after it. He started up the slope, his limp more noticeable during the climb.

Franklin Square was a flat, green oasis above the surrounding streets, studded on this edge with tall eucalyptus trees which smelled like wet dogs. Docker went through the trees and out across the worn grass toward the restrooms. They were set under a dozen young evergreens on the far side of the park, toward Potrero Street.

A black boy and a black girl with wildly exaggerated Afros, both wearing slacks and velvet-trimmed high-heeled boots, were arguing about another girl the boy had taken home the night before. A white hippie chick with a blue bedroll beside her was leaned back against one of the trees as if she were exhausted. Her eyes were shut and her face wan; from the roach between her fingers drifted the harsh scent of burning grass into the clear air.

When Docker was halfway across the grassy area, the youth with the bandido mustache appeared at the top of the slope. He went through the trees, started out into the open as Docker reached the distant restrooms. His mustache, color, and facial features made it impossible to tell whether he was of Negro or Spanish blood.

He started trotting when Docker emerged from the restroom and disappeared around the far side of the small stucco building. He went around the corner fast. But Docker had waited, his back against the notice someone had spray-canned on the wall beside the phone booth: SYLVA CAN ASS IS VISITACION VALLEY'S SLUT!

Docker seized double handfuls of the boy's fleece-lined carcoat and slammed him up against the phone booth, hard enough so the back of his head starred the glass. Only thin crisscrosses of embedded wire kept the glass from breaking.

"Jesus, man, what—"

"You followed me up from Bryant Street," said Docker almost dreamily. He lifted the dark youth so the toes of his boots just touched the ground and held him that way, jammed back against the side of the dark green phone booth. "Talk to me."

"Man, I was just . . . you know . . ."

The youth's eyes were watering and his nose was running. His arms twitched. Docker giggled suddenly and set him back on his feet.

"What are you on?"

"Smack. I figgered . . . When I seen you go into the can . . ."

"There's a pusher working this park?"

"Right, man." The hype was sweating. His eyes dart-

ed first one way and then the other. "It's my connection's turf, man, dig, but he got busted. But I heard
someone was takin' over, so I waited."

Docker broke into sudden laughter. It was a high,
nervous laugh edged with paranoia, which didn't go with
his earlier calm. He said, "There's a dead man over in
seventeen-forty-eight. There's another man there, unconscious. There'll be money in their pockets. In the
bathroom is a twenty-mill ampule of speed you can sell
for more bread. The key's in the mailbox. Get moving."

The young addict was staring, wide-eyed. "What are
you tellin' me, man?" he exclaimed in alarm. "What are
you tryina do to me?"

"Up to you," said Docker.

He was still laughing. He seemed to have a hard time
stopping. The laughter had tones of hysteria in it. He
stood with his hands in his topcoat pockets and the
attaché case between his feet, watching the hype edge
away around the corner of the building. When he had
disappeared, Docker quit laughing. His face looked as if
it had never known laughter of any kind.

He fished a dime out of his pocket. After he had used
it, he caught a bus.

Two

The phone was ringing in the empty office when Pamela
Gardner unlocked the street door. On the inside of the
glass in capital letters were the words NEIL FARGO and
underneath in smaller caps, INVESTIGATIONS; Pamela
was carrying a newspaper, her brown-bagged lunch, the
current doorstop from Book of the Month, and a dress
in a large cardboard box which she was returning to

House of Nines after work. She was a tiny girl barely five feet tall, perhaps 95 pounds in weight.

"Coming," she muttered as she fought to get her key back from the door.

The ringing phone hurried her, however, so she dropped first the Book of the Month, then, in retrieving it, the dress. She finally left them to run up the narrow straight stairs to the second-floor office. Her skirt was short enough so she would have been showing a great deal of pantyhose to anyone climbing the steps behind her. Her thighs still had a slight adolescent chunkiness which was somehow rather innocent.

The phone stopped ringing just as she picked it up. "Oh, damn!"

She had rescued her packages, had begun distributing items into drawers, on desk and file cabinet tops in the time-honored secretarial ritual, when the phone started ringing again.

"Neil Fargo, Investigations."

Still wearing her coat, she took the message, hung up. The phone immediately began ringing again.

"Neil Fargo, Investigations."

She took another message, got out of her coat and got the coffee started. She always cleaned the pot before leaving the office at night. She was around twenty, with a short nose and a long upper lip. Her eyes were blue, very bright, wide-set. Given five more years and five fewer pounds, the right clothes and a different hair style, she would be a beautiful woman. Right now she was a perky kid with a trim figure a little too wide in the hips for her diminutive size, her small, pointed breasts softened by a furry pale yellow sweater.

Twelve minutes later, at 8:19, the street door admitted Neil Fargo. He came up the stairs two at a time, whistling cheerily. Pamela was reading the morning *Chronicle*, since there had been no reports on the dictating machine.

"Any calls?"

"Maxwell Stayton's secretary will expect you when Mr. Stayton arrives at ten." She made a face, either for Mr. Stayton or his secretary but probably the latter. "Two calls from that importer down on Battery Street, Walter Hariss; he'll drop by personally. One from a man named Docker, no message, and—"

"Docker?" demanded Neil Fargo sharply.

His direct brown eyes had gotten surprisingly bleak. He was a big, blocky man with an angular, somewhat Indian face and nondescript brown hair cut subtly shorter than current styles. It made his face almost brutal in the way that Burt Lancaster's once was brutal, although he looked nothing at all like Lancaster.

"No first name or initial." She suddenly giggled, betraying her youth. "He had a mushy voice, like he had false teeth."

"He leave a number?"

"Said he'd call back." But something in his voice had sobered her. She looked up at him with bright blue eyes alive to nuance. Her face was narrow, narrow-chinned, all the features fine and sharp as good portraiture. "Is something the matter, Neil? Who is Docker?"

Neil Fargo tapped lightly on the edge of her desk with his knuckles. He smiled. The smile made the hard, bony face less stark even though he did not have the sort of features that a smile particularly enhanced.

"If Docker calls back, try to get a number."

"Neil . . ." She paused, troubled, then said in a rush, "This doesn't have anything to do with Walter Hariss, does it?"

"Why?"

She made a small, meaningless gesture. "I've heard he . . . People say he imports more than cheap pottery and tourist curios. And that Docker mentioned his name. Something about getting to you before Hariss did."

"Docker and Hariss?" Neil Fargo was not totally successful in making the idea sound new to him. He said, "You'll be a detective yet, doll."

He went into his small private office set off from the main room by head-high partitions. The windows looked down on the intersection of Bush and Franklin Streets. Neil Fargo took off his topcoat. He was wearing a dark blue double-knit suit and a white shirt with a wide dark tie that gave him a substantial, conservative air. He set the dusty Venetian blinds so he could look out the windows.

By the time he had drunk a cup of black coffee and smoked one cigarette, Walter Hariss had arrived. Neil Fargo smiled without mirth, watching the importer get out of the rear seat of the black Fleetwood his nasty little chauffeur had maneuvered into a slot halfway up Bush Street.

Neil Fargo went to the open door of his office, which offered privacy from his secretary only with the door shut. He leaned against the frame with his arms folded. The two men clattered up the stairs.

"You've met my secretary, Pamela Gardner," said Neil Fargo. He made' appropriate gestures. "Pamela, Gus Rizzato—Mr. Hariss' chauffeur."

Hariss followed him into the inner office, then after Neil Fargo had sat down behind the desk, said, "This is private."

The detective nodded amiably and went to the door again. Gus Rizzato was beside Pamela's chair, leaning down to say something to her. He was built like a jockey and had black hair and a swarthy face with a bad complexion. His tie was six inches wide, just barely wider than the lapels on his suit. The girl was shaking her head at what he was saying, making her short brown hair dance around her temples. Her face was set and pale.

"Will you go downstairs to Stempel's and get us some doughnuts, doll?" The girl nodded hurriedly and stood up. Neil Fargo added, "And then go over to the Seventy-Six station and tell Emil to fill up the Fairlane. Don't hurry."

"Yes, Mr. Fargo." There was relief in her voice.

She got her purse and started down the stairs. Rizzato looked appreciatively after her. He winked at Neil Fargo, made obscene gestures that crudely suggested sexual intercourse, and swaggered out after the girl.

Neil Fargo stared after him, then returned to the cubicle where Hariss waited impatiently.

"Sometime I'm going to do something about that little son of a bitch," he said to the importer.

Walter Hariss made a dismissive gesture with his hand. He was a small-boned, solid man in his late forties, with a good tan and a round, slightly fleshy face and full lips, who wore very expensive clothes well. He wore his grey hair medium length, brushed back from his face in a modified pompadour. His shoes gleamed. Only the overripe diamond on his pinky finger destroyed the illusion of solid businessman.

Neil Fargo sighed and nodded. "All right. What went wrong?"

"We got knocked over."

"Knocked over!" The detective's thin lips tightened into a wolfish grin, emphasizing the Indian cast of his features. He made it an exclamation, not a question.

"At the drop point. My courier, Julio Marquez, got killed and my chemist got laid out. And then the cops showed up before he could get out."

"Tipped," muttered Neil Fargo.

He got up, paced twice back and forth beside the desk, cracking his fisted right hand into his left palm.

"Your fucking friend Docker is missing and so is my kilo of H," said Hariss. "To say nothing of the attaché case."

"Docker called here before I got in. Docker. Hah!" He struck the desk suddenly with the flat of his palm. His calender jumped an inch off the polished hardwood. His eyes got mean. "Well, you're the fucker who wanted everything done through intermediaries. Didn't want to be there yourself. Didn't want me there. A hundred and seventy-five thousand bucks was in that attaché case and I'm responsible to the money man for it!"

"Was there?" asked Hariss. His pale eyes burned softly in his ruddy face. He had a well-modulated voice that suggested he had spent quite a lot of time learning to speak well.

"What the fuck's that supposed to mean?"

"You're the one came up with Docker as the drop man. Old Army buddy from Vietnam, would lick the sweat off your balls for you." He leaned closer. He jabbed Neil Fargo in the stomach with the forefinger of the hand that held his dollar cigar. "Maybe you just kept the money, told your buddy to knock off the courier and Addison, my chemist, and—"

"Sure," said Neil Fargo in a savage voice. "We plan murder in an apartment I rent in my own name that has my fingerprints all over it so the police will be sure to know where to look. Quit fucking around. I'm on the hook to the money man, Hariss!"

"Who *is* the money man?"

Neil Fargo just shook his head. "How did you get onto this so fast? The seven o'clock news?"

"It was a phone tip, one of the prowlies who responded called me, he owed me a favor and knew I used Addison. He said there was a pottery figure broken on the floor—you know what that means."

"And no attaché case," muttered Neil Fargo.

"I asked my man about that, casually. That's when he remembered he saw someone getting on a Bryant Street bus with an attaché case. Just as they were pulling up. He didn't know it was important at the time."

"Observant cop," said Neil Fargo. "Any description?"

"Big man, long blond hair, glasses—that's your fucking Docker, right?"

Neil Fargo nodded sourly. "Docker."

"Do you know where to find him? Where he'd go? What he'd do?"

"He's only been in town three weeks—he was supposed to be staying in that apartment." He took his nervous turn around the little office again. "Christ, Hariss, he needed the money, he looked right for this. He was square with me in Nam, kept me from getting my ass shot off a couple of times."

Precision lent heavy menace to the importer's voice. His gestures wreathed his head in cigar smoke.

"I want that fucker, Fargo. A quarter of a million in smack in that clay figure, and—"

"Street prices," said Neil Fargo almost contemptuously. "I figure you paid maybe twelve, thirteen thou for it in Mexico. *If* it was ninety-five percent pure, as you claimed."

"*Your* chemist."

"I had a chemist there in good faith—"

Walter Hariss suppressed whatever he had been going to say. He stood up. He was a stocky five-eight, the top of his razor-cut grey hair came to Neil Fargo's upper lip. He put an arm around the detective's broad shoulders. He found a smile that cost him something extra.

"We don't have to fight, Neil. We both want the same thing, right? The money back, the heroin back. You—"

He broke off as the street door opened, closed; Pamela's light, nervously cheery tones came up the stairwell ahead of the sound of her heels on the stairs.

"Find Docker, we'll get the rest of it straightened out," said Neil Fargo hurriedly. "Have Alex Kolinski get his street people on Docker, and add to the description that he's got a slight limp—knicked in the right knee in Nam. Partial disability. I'll start at the other end—phone, utilities, driver's license, the usual skiptracing routines."

He stood aside for Hariss to leave first, trailing aromatic cigar smoke. Outside, Pamela Gardner was back behind her desk, the white paper bag of doughnuts on the blotter in front of her. She looked as if the desk were a breached redoubt. Gus Rizzato was sitting on the edge of it, one hand on her shoulder, talking earnestly. In talking, he used eyebrows and mouth and his entire mobile Latin countenance. He looked up at the detective and grinned.

"I like this little girl, Fargo. Why don't you tell her it wouldn't be a bad idea for her to act a little more friendly?"

Neil Fargo said heartily to Hariss, "Good to have you drop by, Walt. I think we can clear up that little matter today."

Then his long arm shot out and his big hand gathered in the front of Rizzato's shirt, tie and jacket lapels as well. The arm twitched. It jerked Rizzato off the desk and slammed him down on his feet like snapping a towel in a locker room.

"You put any more hands on that girl, Peeler, I'll break them off." His voice and mouth were cool, contemptuous. His eyes were hot and vicious. He let go of the shirt front and stepped back.

Rizzato measured him icily, on the edge of violence, though he was at least a foot shorter than the detective. Hariss said sharply, "Gus."

Rizzato's fighting-dog stance relaxed. He straightened his jacket with a pompous shrug, strutted out of the office like a jockey who can no longer make the weight. Hariss followed.

When the street door closed behind them, the girl, who had been sitting very straight in her chair, put her hands up to her cheeks. Crimson suddenly flushed across her features.

"He said to me . . . He told me he wanted to . . ."

"Sorry I let him in here, doll."

She started to say something more, stopped, then took down her hands from her face. The flush was receding. She said, "Why did you call him Peeler?"

"The story goes that he was once assigned to shut up somebody who was talking to an assistant D.A. back East . . ." He broke off. He said tonelessly, "You don't really want to know."

"I do." Her eyes were bright again.

"The story goes he took this guy down into a basement in Brooklyn and skinned him alive."

The girl made a choked sound in her throat and her flush receded further, so her face was almost pale.

"You asked," said Neil Fargo. He was bent over the desk writing rapidly on her scratch pad. As he wrote, he talked. "Docker. Here's everything I have on him, which isn't a hell of a lot. I want the full drill, doll. DMV check for license and possible auto registration, credit check, phone company, our contacts at the gas company and scavengers. I want to know if he's bottled up here in town, or if he made it out. Airlines, train, buses. If he doesn't have a car, start a run on the car-rental places. Private charter plane services—you know the routine. If the police call, I went out, you don't know where."

"Police?"

"That's the way it is. Friend Docker put me in the middle."

"Between Walt Hariss and who?" she said bitterly. "Nobody ate any doughnuts and your car didn't need any gas."

Neil Fargo laid a hand on her cheek, knuckles to the flesh, ran it back toward her ear like someone playing with a cat. Her eyes went very slightly unfocussed. He went back into his own office, shut the door, sat at the desk, dialled a number he didn't have to look up. Through the closed door he could hear Pamela dialling also on the other line, starting the skiptracing routine on Docker.

The phone was picked up, but whoever had picked it up did nothing except breathe into it. Neil Fargo said, "Your money's been hijacked."

The breathing arrested. "Hijacked?"

"This morning."

"I thought you told me that money would buy me—"

"Forget what I told you."

"I see." There was a pause. "Would it be asking too much to know how that amount of cash money was placed in a position where it *could* be hijacked?"

"I trusted somebody I shouldn't have. A man named Docker. He saved my life in Vietnam, but now . . ."

"I wonder why I should trust *you*, Fargo."

The detective ignored the remark. "There's another complication. At the same time your money got lifted, a man got killed."

"Who? Where? Did this man Docker—"

"I'll know more when the police catch up with me."

"Police? How do they know you have anything?"

"I rented the place where it happened—in my own name. I didn't expect anything like a killing there."

After a longer pause, the voice said, "How vulnerable are you?"

"I'll get by," said Neil Fargo. "I'll be in touch."

He hung up. He sat with his hands still on the phone for a few seconds, frowning. There was a light sheen of sweat on his forehead although it was not particularly hot in the office. He stood up, flipped his topcoat over his arm, picked up a briefcase from beside the desk. He stopped at Pamela Gardner's desk. Her scratch pad was open to a new sheet, and scribbled notations already covered it.

"If Docker calls again, get a phone number out of him."

"Neil," she almost wailed. "Why? You promised you'd go down to the city assessor's office today to get a lead on Maxwell Stayton's daughter. That's clean money. It isn't dangerous. Why can't you—"

"And so I shall, doll," he said soothingly. "But meanwhile, if you get anything important on Docker, leave a message with Stayton's secretary. I'll be getting over there eventually to report. See, I *am* working on his case. I expect something to break on it today."

She said bitterly, "While you're off—"

He grinned and touched her under the chin. "You're a lovely, romantic little nut. But if all I did was look for Roberta Stayton when she runs off threatening to marry some flake, neither of us would eat. Docker, doll. It *is* important."

He went out.

Three

Age had shrunken the door from its frame, so it rattled discreetly under the timid knuckles. Alex Kolinski, fully clothed from the waist up, paid no attention. Instead, he spoke to the girl kneeling beside the ancient, broken-down double bed.

"Keep it up, bitch," he said in a monotone, as if training a dog. The timid knuckles sounded against the door again.

"Mr. Kolinski?" The voice from the hall was female, Negro south, frightened. "It's the telephone, Mr. Kolinski. It's . . . Mr. Hariss, Mr. Kolinski."

Kolinski looked up unwillingly, like a man disturbed in the midst of an absorbing book. He had a prognathous jaw and heavy ridges of bone around the eyes, making them deep-set. But it was not a stupid face, nor was there anything Neanderthal about his body. The neck which supported the hominid face was surprisingly unmassive.

"Mr. Kolinski . . ."

"All right, goddammit!" he burst out. "Tell him . . ."

A sudden spasm of cruel ecstasy stilled his voice. He plunged his hands into the thick, lifeless hair of the girl on her knees beside the bed. Dandruff speckled the scalp around the center part.

"Oh, yeah! That's it!" exploded Kolinski in a hoarse, thickened voice.

From the hall came the timid rapping again. "Mr. Kolinski, he . . . he said it was important."

But Kolinski was finished. He stood up to dry himself with a corner of the sheet. The girl stared up at him from eyes which looked huge in her famished countenance. She had a face that had once been astonishingly beautiful. Even now, haggard and drawn, it was patrician of nose and striking of facial bone. A thoroughbred face. The eyes were dark, very dark-circled also, wet with tears even though they met his gaze without shame.

"Alex, can I have it now?"

Kolinski standing above her like a sated storm trooper, jerked his belt tight. "I've got a phone call."

"But afterwards, Alex." An almost childish hope of reward curved her thin lips. "Afterwards you'll let me have it."

"We'll see, bitch."

The girl put her face down in her arms, like an exhausted distance runner. The arms were thin. She was dressed in a shapless flannel nightgown so only her long narrow well-shaped feet, bare against the cold linoleum floor, were visible.

"Alex, please, you promised . . ." When he stepped away without answering, she raised her head from her arms to cry after him, "Alex, *please!*"

He paused in the doorway to look back at her. He laughed.

"Sweat, bitch," he said.

He went out.

The girl remained motionless after he had gone. Finally, she climbed wearily to her feet, like a housewife summoned by the phone in the middle of scrubbing the kitchen floor. She was tall and would once have been fashionably slender, now was angular and thin under the washed-out, faded nightdress. Despite her height, she could not have weighed as much as Pamela Gardner.

She walked back and forth in the center of the room with quick, jerky strides. Her face worked with passion or pain. She stopped abruptly in mid-stride to stare at the single straight-backed chair which, with the bed and the narrow, gaudily pink dresser, gave the room its only furniture.

Kolinski's three-hundred-dollar overcoat was tossed carelessly over the back of the chair.

"Oh, thank God! Thank God!" the girl exclaimed in a low voice.

She bent over the coat to stroke it with an almost feline motion, like a cat licking its paw so it can wash its face. She did not try to go through the pockets. Instead, she turned away quickly to the dresser.

From the top drawer she got a white candle stub about three inches long. She lit it, dripped wax on the top of the dresser next to myriad shiny places where other blobs of wax had been scraped away. Next to the candle she laid a blackened tablespoon with the handle bent in a crude S-shape, and an empty ten-cc syringe with the needle already attached.

The girl went back to the bed, sat down on the edge of it where Kolinski had sat. Sitting, she fidgeted and shivered. Only muscles standing out along the side of her narrow jaw like molded strips of putty kept her teeth from chattering. Her face looked aged under the lank, sweat-dampened hair. Her sweat had a sweetish smell, like the dried sweat in dancers' leotards not laundered often enough.

Sitting there, waiting, she kept monotonously flexing her left hand like an athlete squeezing a handball to strengthen his fingers. Twice she stopped to look anxiously at the veins inside the elbow, where the masses of scar tissue from needle tracks were. Some of the more recent tracks were ulcerated. She had long since stopped using Preparation H in an effort to shrink and minimize the marks.

The girl gave a low moan of either pain or frustration. The skin was so calloused that the veins had not really come up beneath it.

She extended the arm, palm up, and began gently slapping the scarred inner elbow with the fingertips of her right hand. The left hand kept spasmodically flexing as she did. Frustrated need made her hips writhe slowly on the bed in a terrible travesty of sexual arousal.

The veins did not come up. The girl started to cry.

Down the hall, standing at the pay phone and listening to the voice of Walter Hariss, Alex Kolinski was scratching his ass through his trousers. Twice he tried to interrupt. When he finally made it, he talked so fast that little flecks of spittle dotted the black plastic of the phone and the grey peeling wall behind it.

"I don't give a shit about your long view or your overall plans on this, Walt. You and I have had different aims from the beginning. That's all right, we've been able to work around that. But you're the one who insisted we bring that fucking Neil Fargo into it, because you thought you could milk him for info about old man Stayton and to give yourself protection at the same time. Protection!" He spat out the word. "Sure, you're protected. And also we don't have any fucking . . ." He checked himself over the word he had been going to use, said, "merchandise," and went on, "to sell, and no additional capital to . . ."

He stopped. He had to, Walter Hariss was talking again. Kolinski listened for perhaps thirty seconds, nodding impatiently, then broke in again.

"All right, sure, Fargo would say that whether he was

in it with his fucking buddy Docker or not. And besides—" He broke off, said in a different voice, "Wait a
sec . . ."

He lowered the receiver so he could look to his left.
The pay phone was in the narrow first-floor hall of the
flophouse, just a few feet from the office door. The office
itself was a square cell with a waist-high glass-front cage
much like a theater ticket-taker's case. Chicken wire was
embedded in the glass, which had a round hole cut
through it at head-height for talking. The glass could be
slid up from inside for the passage of money across the
counter.

"Hey you!" yelled Kolinski. "Aunt Jemima!"

Behind the hole in the glass appeared the face of a
beady-eyed black girl in her early twenties. She had
short frizzled black hair that gleamed wetly under the
office's single strong unshaded bulb. It was a round,
rather pushed-down face with very thick lips covered
with incongruous coral-red lipstick. It was a young face
which already could have been surprised by nothing except kindness.

"Yes, sir, Mr. Kolinski?"

"Go downstairs and check the mail."

"But Mr. Kolinski, mail was delivered an hour ago!
Ain't gonna be no more mail in that box now jes'
cause—"

"Get to fuck down there!" yelled Kolinski.

A pink tongue came out over the fat coral lips. The
face disappeared, to reappear in a few moments after
the heavy hardwood door beside the glass cage had
opened. This had been accompanied by the rattling of
withdrawn deadbolts. The girl waddled out. She had on
a short skirt that showed fat black thighs above dimpled
knees. Under ther dirty pink sweater were bulbous
breasts as firm as cows' udders.

"I goin', Mist' Kolinski." In her nervousness, her
speech regressed to North Carolina or perhaps Georgia.

Kolinski stood stock-still with the receiver in his hand
as she waddled by. She went down the narrow stairwell.
Kolinski watched her retreat in the round fly-specked
mirror set at an angle above the turn of the stairs. He

watched her all the way down to street level. Watched her pull open the street door and go out.

He lifted the receiver, resumed his staccato delivery as if there had been no interruption.

"Just getting rid of the nigger. And besides, you may be protected but I'm hanging out in the wind with my dick flopping. I've worked like a fucking dog getting a street distribution system set up—"

"Nobody could have worked harder, Alex," said Hariss' voice smoothly.

"It's what I'm telling you. My half of this one-seven-five, placed with our Mexican distributor for more merchandise, would have been worth nearly a mil on the street, and I—"

"You talk as if that money is gone."

"Isn't it?"

"I'm at the Bush Street garage, I took the liberty of telling Blaney to set your street people into operation before I saw Fargo. They're covering the depots. Of course if Docker has a car—"

"Fargo will find that out soon enough—if Fargo is playing straight with us."

"As we're playing straight with Fargo?" Hariss chuckled at his own remark. Kolinski ignored it; his face had gotten thoughtful. Intelligence gleamed in his deep-set eyes.

"But if he had a car, he wouldn't have had to take a fucking bus away from Bryant Street, would he? No, Walt, goddammit, I think he's holed up somewhere! Shit, that much . . . merchandise, he can only dispose of it here or in L.A. or in Seattle. He couldn't find buyers with enough bread anywhere else."

"If he stays on the coast."

"They'd eat him alive back East, and I think he's smart enough to know it. Shit, he was smart enough to knock us over."

"Exactly what I've been telling you, Alex. I think we've a very good chance of recouping. I'll expect you at Bush Street in a few minutes to direct operations."

Four

Kolinski went back down the narrow hall in long strides. The walls were grey, peeling paint, the rug grey with pink flowers and getting threadbare in the center, patterned in a design which was like animal guts dumped on a slaughter-house floor. At the last room, just before the fifteen-watt red bulb marking the alley firestairs, Kolinski turned in.

He crossed the girl's room in his long strides, swept up his overcoat from the chair, thrust his arms into the sleeves. As he swung back toward the door, she scrambled off the bed. She was white-faced.

"Alex!" she cried. "Please! You promised—"

"I don't have the time, bitch—"

She threw thin arms around his neck, clung to him with the strength of desperation. "I . . . wasn't I good this morning?"

He pushed her back against the wall, then paused momentarily. Seeing the indecision in his face, she returned to him like a struck dog to its master, fawning but undaunted. Her mouth was ingratiating, her voice determinedly seductive.

"Wasn't I, Alex?"

"You were good, Robin," he said finally. "A good little sow, lapping it up. Here." His hand brought three small glassine envelopes out of his inner suit jacket pocket. He dropped them on the bed. He watched the girl scrabble frantically at them with an oddly erotic look on his face. "They'll keep you until tomorrow."

The girl was between him and the door again. Her face, her voice, her emaciated body pleaded her cause.

"Alex, can't you . . . Please."

21

"Jesus!" he burst out in a softly angry voice.

"You know how I hate to shoot myself up, Alex."

"Look, I've got problems, I've got . . ."

He stopped there. A thoughtful look had entered his eyes. He stood still watching her shake heroin into the spoon, add water from the ancient single-tap sink in the corner.

She moved the spoon carefully over the candle flame until the water and drug had gone into solution. Despite her desperate need, the girl's movements were efficient, swift, sure. Kolinski watched the process as if mesmerized. She filled the syringe and handed it to him needle-up like a nurse in a TV medical show.

The girl returned to the bed, lay back against the pillows. He sat down beside her. She was working on her veins again. Kolinski watched her, avidly now. He had another erection.

"You really love it, don't you?" he asked her.

Her huge dark eyes, intent on her hands, answered his question. Then her need overcame her, she seized the short sleeve of her nightdress with her right hand and twisted it so the tight edge of the sleeve bit cruelly into the thin upper arm. This finally brought up the vein.

"Little Robin," said Kolinski softly. "The early bird who eats the worm." He laughed. He slid the needle into her arm. "My worm. Whenever I want you to."

"Oh, yes, Alex, whenever you want me to . . ."

Kolinski depressed the plunger a couple of centimeters, then drew it back. The milky solution in the syringe turned pink as blood was drawn into it. He had made the vein on the first try.

His thumb moved, shoving heroin into her bloodstream. He said, mockingly, "Jesus, baby, if your old man could see you now! I'd love to see your old man's face."

The girl's own face had gotten very intent and serious, like that of a student trying to catch every word of a difficult and involved lecture. She drew in a deep breath as the flash hit her, and the pupils of her eyes changed.

She exclaimed, "Hit me with the rest of it, lover. Let me feel it. Oh!"

Kolinski withdrew the needle, sat with the hypo on his hands. It was empty except for a faintly pink residue in the bottom of the syringe.

"Jesus, a hype who hates to shoot herself up!" He shook his head in wonder. The change in the girl was almost miraculous. Her voice was light, almost coquettish.

"There's a lot of us hate to do it ourselves, Alex!"

"All of them women."

She pouted. "We just don't like the needle."

"You like the dick. In the mouth." He laughed heavily, tossed the syringe on the bed beside her and stood up. "I notice you're quick enough to shoot yourself up when nobody else is around."

Robin made a moue with her beautifully-shaped mouth. She looked her real age, a malnutritioned thirty-one or -two, instead of the raddled fifty she had looked a few minutes before. She smiled. Her eyes sparkled.

Kolinski's erection had subsided. He said, "Listen, I got to get back to Bush Street but I want you to do something for me."

"Anything," she said simply. She drew up her legs under the worn nightdress and clasped her arms around them. She rested her chin on her knees in a listening attitude.

"There's a guy in town, has been here a couple, three weeks, anyway long enough to have maybe needed a woman. We want him bad. Goes by the name of Docker. He's a big guy with . . ."

He stopped there because the girl's face had changed, utterly. She had swung her legs off the bed and had suddenly stood up. Her voice was very excited.

"You said *Docker*? A big guy, six feet, six-one? Horn-rim glasses and long blond—"

Kolinski had her by the upper arms, was squeezing them so hard that she looked momentarily faint.

"You *know* him? Has a limp—"

"One of the girls. He was with one of the girls a couple of nights ago. She said he was a son of a bitch, used a belt on her until she screamed. He told her it was the only way he could be sure she was really interested."

"How are you sure of the name?"

"She snooped his wallet after he'd fallen asleep. She said he had a lot of money in there but she was afraid to take any. She said when he woke up he checked."

"Who was it? Which girl?"

Robin opened her mouth, then frowned and shut it. She shook her head. "I can't remember, we were all having coffee down on the corner and . . ." Her face brightened. "I'll find out today for you, Alex. I'll find out everything she remembers that might help. I know he took her to his apartment because he wanted her all night. I can get the address, anyway."

He had her by the arms again. His face was elated, but his voice was solemn. "Robin, you turn that son of a bitch for me and I'll put you in a hype's paradise. I mean it! As much as you want, as often as you want it."

Kolinski went back down the hall to the front desk, but he still did not leave, even though it had been nearly fifteen minutes since Hariss had said he was expecting him immediately. Instead, he stopped by the telephone and called, "Hey, Aunt Jemima!"

The office door opened and the chubby black girl appeared. If she resented either his words or his tone, it didn't show on her face. Kolinski smiled at her.

"Was there any mail downstairs?"

"No, sir, Mr. Kolinski."

Kolinski crowded her back against the wall. His right hand came up between their bodies, with a lover's gentleness cupped as much of one of the immense breasts as his fingers could span.

"This is important, Aunt Jemima. You didn't take any phone calls from Mr. Hariss for me this morning, did you?"

The girl was staring intently up into his face, wide-eyed, her ebony features shiny with dread. She shook her head quickly. "No, sir, Mr. Kolinski, I most surely didn't!"

"Surely didn't what?"

"Take any phone calls from Mr. Har—"

As she spoke the name, Kolinski's fingers twisted viciously like someone turning up time on a parking meter. The girl screamed once before she was able to get the back of one hand up to her face. She bit down hard on it to cut off any further sounds. Her eyes never left Kolinski's face. No doors opened to her cry.

Kolinski, still smiling, let his hand slide down her body and stepped back. The girl was shuddering against the wall, but made no move to touch her brutalized breast. The physical stench of her fear was palpable between them.

"Surely didn't what?" repeated Kolinski.

"I . . . There was no phone calls for you this morning, Mr. Kolinski."

"And?"

"You weren't here this morning, sir."

Kolinski smiled delightedly. He laid a finger gently against the black girl's fat carmined lips. He said, "I'll bet you give a mean blowjob with a mouth like that, honey."

"Ye . . . yes, sir, Mr. Kolinski."

He said thoughtfully, "Maybe one of these days . . ."

"Yes, sir, Mr. Kolinski." She paused. "Thank you, Mr. Kolinski."

Back in her room, Robin had remained standing beside the bed, exactly as Kolinski had left her, for a full thirty seconds. Then she crossed swiftly to the door, pulled it open a foot and cautiously thrust her head out. Past his waiting back, at the far end of the hall, she could see the black girl just emerging from the office.

Robin shut the door, twisted the key in the lock, then went to the bureau for a clean handkerchief. Her movements, with the craving temporarily stilled within her, were unconsciously graceful and fluid. Her habit was heavy enough that five cc's of the street-strength solution were merely sufficient to restore her to a normal behavioral state, not enough to put her on the nod. She was humming to herself. Her eyes danced with a fierce joy that was like anger.

With the handkerchief around her fingers, and using a feather touch, she picked up the syringe from the bed where Kolinski had tossed it. Her fingers gripped it with the clean linen just at the very base of the barrel, where the needle fitted over it. She turned the syringe this way and that under the unshaded bulb hanging by its bare cord from the converted gas fixture in the ceiling.

Whatever the light showed her made Robin smile in satisfaction. She carried the syringe over to the bureau, opened a drawer, nested the syringe lovingly in the handkerchief. She was just shutting the drawer when the black girl's scream came up the hall to freeze her movements.

She waited. The cry was not repeated. She hurriedly blew out the candle, but did not remove it. She went to the wash basin, took up toothpaste and brush from the stained and yellowed enamel, began to brush her teeth very methodically, as if she could never get the inside of her mouth clean.

Only then did Robin cross to the door, unlock it, look out again. The hallway was deserted. On bare silent feet, leaving her door wide behind her, she padded down to the office. The black girl was sitting behind the tiny desk, her immense breasts, bared, flowing halfway across its littered surface. She was crying bitterly.

"Daphne," called the white girl softly.

Daphne raised her head with a stricken, guilty look. Seeing who it was, she knuckled her reddened eyes like a hurt child, grunted to her feet to reach across and open the door. She didn't bother to pull her sweater back down.

"I heard you scream," said Robin. "What . . ."

"That motherfucker Kolinski! He hurt me. See? He took an' twisted my tit, wasn't no call that motherfucker do that."

"Did he hurt you badly?"

"I'll live." The fat lips writhed. "But someday I'm gonna cut that motherfucker's motherfucking nuts off, I swear. Someday . . ."

"Not someday, Daphne. *Now*."

"Now?" Daphne's face had changed. Fear and greed

had entered it, were fighting their age-old battle on her essentially guileless features."

"It's today, Daphne."

"Miss Robin, I know what we done talk about, but—"

Robin came quickly into the office. She shut the door behind her, put an arm around the black girl's meaty shoulders as a mother might. "It's more than talk, Daphne. It's today. This afternoon."

Daphne licked the fat red lips. "An' the money, Miss Robin. It's truly what you said? Five th . . ." Her voice lost the figure when she tried to say it. "Five thousand dollars? Just for—"

"Just for the phone call at exactly the time I told you." The white girl's thin patrician features were expressionless. "That, and sticking to your story afterwards. That's as important as the phone call. Sticking to it even in court."

"An' you'll back up my story?"

Robin smiled as at a secret joke. "Absolutely."

"That motherfucker get out on bail, get hold of my black ass—"

"He won't, Daphne. My . . . testimony will keep him in jail."

The black girl looked at her distrustfully, gave her own fear one more chance before succumbing to greed and hatred. "Where your kinda dope fiend get that kinda money, Miss Robin? You out on the street turning tricks when that motherfucker don't give you your fix, where you gonna get—"

"I'll have it, Daphne. I'll put five thousand dollars on the corner of my dresser. After the phone call, come down and get it." Her eyes and voice changed. "I'll be on the nod. I won't see you take it, but don't try to change your story afterwards. If you do . . ."

"I know," said Daphne glumly. "You got friends. Every motherfucker in this world got friends, 'cept Daphne."

"By tonight you'll have five thousand friends, Daphne."

The black girl's eyes suddenly glittered. "Yeah!" she exclaimed softly. "Five thousand bucks! I fix that motherfucker. I fix that motherfucker's honky ass good!"

The white girl went back down the hall to her room. She shut but did not lock the door. She looked at the cheap alarm clock on top of the dresser, lay down on the bed on her back. It was a bit past ten o'clock. The heroin was still at work in her. She lay there quietly, a junkie whore named Robin on a whore's sprung bed in a cheap junkie whore's slovenly room.

She waited.

Five

As Robin waited, the search for Docker was spreading across San Francisco. Not the San Francisco famous to tourists for the 49-Mile Drive, the bright flower stall on the Bank of America's sprawling dark plaza, the St. Francis Hotel's dizzying exterior elevators to the tower. Not even the San Francisco of the rich condominiums of Russian and Nob Hills, or of the rows of boxy tracts which had stilled the once-restless sands of the Sunset District.

But San Francisco all the same, a real city as valid as the one they shoot movies in, and give awards to the restaurants of, and write books about.

An underbelly San Francisco, in which Alex Kolinski was on his way to the Bush Street parking garage where Walter Hariss waited, smoking an impatient cigar. In which Pamela Gardner was on the phone, skiptracing the big blond man named Docker. Neil Fargo was just parking his Fairlane in the Fifth and Mission garage. And a uniformed prowlie named Edmunds had feigned sudden illness and had, on behalf of his monthly pay-off from Walter Hariss, tracked down the driver of the 25 Bryant bus which had carried Docker to Army Street. There the big blond-haired, limping man with the attaché case had debussed, and there the trail had ended.

For the moment. But the city through which Docker now moved had thousands of watching eyes and outstretched hands. This was the muggers' and pushers' and prosties' and hypes' San Francisco. The city of cab drivers so stoned on grass that the shadow line between reality and dream became a little tenuous even on shift. The city of black kids who shot out the windows of Hunters Point buses for fun, of militants who raided precinct police stations with automatic weapons for real, and of Chinatown juvies from the Chung Ching Yee, Hwa Ching, and Suey Sing gangs who emptied .22's into one another for an illusory concept of territory.

It was the city of cheap hustlers like Rowlands, one of many street types alerted by Kolinski's lieutenant to watch for a big mean cat with long blond hair and a limp and some sort of briefcase. Rowlands was a round little man who made a vague living off information picked up here and there concerning this and that.

He had taken up his post inside the front doors of the Greyhound Terminal on Seventh Street just south of Market. His hands were in his pockets and he was staring blankly out at the taxi rank like a man waiting for his wife, teetering from one foot to the other, checking his Timex. But his deceptively sleepy eyes missed nothing that might translate into money.

At about the same time Rowlands yawned and watched the backside of a girl wobbling down Seventh in a tight skirt, a thin black man named Browne was arriving at the Trailways Bus depot. This was located in the echoing lower level of the East Bay Terminal on First Street, six long blocks away from the Greyhound depot and also just south of Market. Browne wore, among other items of dress, old oxblood dress shoes with a neat hole cut through each upper to ease the corns on his little toes.

Browne looked up First Street and he looked down First Street. His sad brown eyes finally lingered on the phone booth a dozen steps away. His lips moved in silent self-communion. But even though it was a day of bright sunshine, with only a few clouds, it was also October. The phone booth was in shadow. First Street was windy. The wind was cold.

Browne used the crosswalk to get to the Fun Terminal, so placed across from the bus terminal as to catch the eye of servicemen arriving from Treasure Island or the Oakland Army Terminal. Browne bought a fin's worth of dimes from the rock-faced woman in the Fun Terminal's change booth, and chose a pinball machine which happened to give its player a good view of First Street. This included a good view of the Trailways entrance across from the arcade's open portals.

Browne began playing his pinball machine, very slowly, very methodically, making each dime last. Hustlers do not have expense accounts.

Nor are hustlers, of course, the only ones who ignore the litter baskets and cross on WAIT. Even Honest John tourists and straight-arrow, tax-paying San Franciscans like to say fuck it once in a while. Poor old straights sometimes like to spend a little money on non-Establishment fun, and hang around topless bars, and porno flicks, and neighborhood bookies. They get sadly mixed-up with cruising rough trade or back-seat whores. In this underbelly San Francisco they get rolled, or get ripped off, or get a dose, or maybe even get unlucky and so get dead.

Therefore, this alternate San Francisco to the city where the little cable cars reach halfway to the stars is also the cops' San Francisco. Maybe especially the cops' San Francisco.

Because cops spend quite a lot of their time with people who get rolled or ripped off or dead. Particularly dead.

Out on Bryant Street a hard-nosed Homicide inspector named Vincent Wylie had finished his part of the proceedings at 1748, where, less than three hours before, a dead Mexican had turned up. Because Wylie was a good cop, he hadn't returned immediately to the Hall when he had finished in the flat where Marquez had died.

Instead he had leisurely snooped over those nine incongruous dwellings dropped there in the middle of the industrial district. And he had noted with interest that one of them had a real-estate office on the ground floor. What more natural place for local landlords to go with their rentals than a local realtor?

Of course there were things against it in this case. It was an extremely unkempt real-estate office, despite innumerable faded signs advertising everything but the Second Coming. There was an announcement that this office PREPARED HERE ONE'S STATE AND FEDERAL INCOME TAX RETURNS. Another boasted of CHOICE RENTALS which were AVAILABLE NOW. This office was willing to sell HOME OWNERS INSURANCE. There was SPANISH SPOKEN HERE.

Since this sign, like the others, was in English, Wylie was not unduly impressed as he entered the realty office from Bryant Street. The shaky-handed early morning drinker behind the desk, the only one present to perform the advertised miracles, almost caught his fingers in his haste to slam shut his bottle drawer.

"Look here," invited Inspector Vincent Wylie.

The ruddy-faced dipso stared at Wylie's shield. He ran the back of an unsteady hand across his mouth, where the razor had missed a triangle of upper lip. His fingernails were dirty. His nose resembled a russet potato. He might have been able to sell a house to a blind man if the blind man couldn't smell booze.

"Ah, lots of excitement up the street, officer."

Wylie said nothing.

"I . . . see that Mex kid they was taking away hanging around here a lot. I useta think he might be, ah, casing me . . ."

Wylie had a Doberman's eyes in a basset's face. He said nothing.

"Ah . . . what's he done, officer?"

"Inspector," said Wylie's mouth. Wylie's pale, pale-lashed eyes said accusingly, boozer. Said, walk soft, boozer. Said, your broker's license won't last long you fuck around with me, boozer. "You handle that property? Seventeen-forty-eight?"

"I'd . . . have to check my files—"

"Three doors away you have to check?"

The eyes peering past the Idaho russet had begun to water. The realtor was sweating. "I . . ."

"You need a drink, go ahead. I'm not the A.B.C."

The realtor found that very funny; certainly much funnier than Wylie found it. The realtor laughed alone, had his drink alone while subsiding into chuckles. He didn't bother with a glass. The booze was going to get his realtor's ticket much quicker than Wylie would.

Wylie drummed his fingers on the desk top. The laughter stopped abruptly.

"Rented it two weeks ago," said the realtor. Neither his voice nor his hands shook any more. "Big guy, he was, said—"

"Two-ten, two-twenty, blond hair and glasses, a limp?"

"Big guy," repeated the realtor. "But . . ." He was shaking his head, finally going through the thin sheaf of current rentals which slumbered in his cardbox. "No limp that I remember, glasses . . . naw."

"The hair is long. Down to here, maybe."

"That I'd remember. No."

"Rented in the name of Docker?" Nothing in Wylie's persistent voice indicated that the realtor's equally persistent denials had been anything but immensely gratifying. The realtor had found the card. He shook his head.

"No Docker. Different fellow, name of Fargo. One month—"

"*Neil* Fargo?"

"That's him."

"Well well well." Wylie's voice was plump with delight. "Now isn't that handsome? Docker mixed up in a possible murder, and Neil Fargo rents the apartment where it happened. And uses his own name, too."

The realtor was grinning at him like a dog who's brought back a stick—delighted without knowing why. The cop went out into the chilly sunshine without appearing to hear the bottle drawer creak open behind him. Wylie was smiling like a man recalling the tagline

of a good dirty joke; even straight cops can be preju-
diced, and not all prejudices involve minorities. Unless
individuals can be considered as the ultimate in minorities.

Six

Docker, object of all this activity, shifted the attaché
case to his left hand and pushed open the heavy door of
the Greyhound depot. He stopped in the over-explicit
heat of the high-ceilinged room, his eyes behind their
hornrims sweeping it as if they had not seen it before.
Greyhound travel advisory, ranks of waiting room
chairs, straight ahead to the buses, ticket windows to the
right.

Docker went right. Brushing past a rotund little man
who seemed to be waiting for his wife, passing beneath
the destination-jammed schedule board to queue up at
one of the windows in the old-fashioned hardwood ticket seller's partition.

"Sir?"

"Seattle."

"One-way or round-trip?"

"Single."

"That'll be thirty-two dollars, sir."

Docker broke a hundred. It raised no comment. He
stuffed the change into a pocket, carelessly, as if it were
cracked corn, and went to the gift shop for a candy bar.
To get there, he had to pass the little man who seemed
to be waiting for his wife while staring moodily up at the
schedule board. His head was tipped back so a roll of
fat creased the back of his neck. The collar of his tan
sport shirt was dirty, as was what could be seen of his
eyes between his sleepy lids.

The next Seattle bus was at 12:30, nearly two hours away. But Docker went up the gentle ramp, which emphasized his limp, to the loading area. It was a long shed-like building with bare yellow wood beams crisscrossed under an arched ceiling. The sides were open for bus-loading, so it was colder than the terminal building.

Despite the chilliness, there was a great coming and going of people in cheap clothes, women in wrinkled print dresses and cloth coats, men in slacks and windbreakers or suits five years out of date. Behind the pastel-painted snackbar was a double row of black plastic lounge chairs with a miniature TV set affixed to one arm of each. Docker chose one, sat down with the attaché case carefully in his lap, fed in coins. The set came on, but Docker's eyes kept busy around the echoing building.

If they saw anything alarming, they did not reflect it. After five minutes, his muscular body had slumped against the plastic.

Dumpy little Rowlands, still wifeless, was standing against the wall near one of the candy machines by this time. He seemed impatient now, a horseplayer waiting for his bookie, perhaps. Twice he looked toward the back of Docker's head, then cast a measuring glance at the bank of pay phones.

With sudden decision—have to place the bet by phone, damn near post time back East—he came off the wall, turned left and went out between the eight-by-eight posts which divided two of the long-haul gates. His face looked irritable, as if he had a rip in the seat of his pants and wasn't sure whether it showed or not.

This route took him between two beat-up double-decker yellow baggage carts and across the diagonal yellow lines marking the bus lanes. It also took him out of Docker's sight. The broad blacktopped area where the buses pulled up was open to Jessie Street, a narrow alley running down the length of the bus terminal from Seventh Street.

Across Jessie, between the end of the broadshouldered squatty Greyhound Express building and its chain-linked parking lot, was a phone booth. Like Rowlands' route, it was out of sight of the double bank of TV lounge chairs where Docker sat.

As soon as the little tubby man had moved from his wall, Docker's heavy pale head had come up. He had brushed the blond hair back from his face, had watched Rowlands out the boarding gate and across the blacktop and out of sight.

Docker stood up, stretched, sauntered away. But not away from the loading area, not down the ramp to the terminal from which he could have reached Seventh Street unobserved. Instead, he went through the loading gate himself, and across the blacktop toward Jessie Street in Rowlands' wake.

Here was the rattle of baggage carts, the roar of motors and throat-clearing of gears and fart of diesels as the buses jockied for their gates. Behind Docker a metallic female voice announced a departure full of drawn-out vowels which made it as incomprehensible as Swahili. A dozen buses were angled nose-first toward the gates to gorge themselves on travellers. A man in grey work clothes squealed open the baggage compartment in the side of one of them and said he would be a son of a bitch, as if he had found sacred mushrooms growing there.

Docker angled across Jessie to the big open sliding metal doors of the Greyhound Express building. Several baggage-handlers were having a smoke. Docker made no attempt to enter the doors, but stopped beside them. One of them was saying, ". . . ol' boy caught me with a pool cue right on the nose and I hit the floor like *that,* man . . ."

"Pardon me," said Docker, "could you—"

"An' then this boy starts puttin' his number nines on me, I mean, man—"

"Could you tell me—"

"Man, he was layin' nothin' but Neolite all over me. He was walkin' up an' down my spine—"

"I'd like to know," said Docker, "if I can get to Mission—"

"I said to him, 'You dam' fool, let me up an' I'll run!' "

Docker laughed with the others, finally getting their attention. He said, "I'd like to get to Mission Street without going out to Seventh. Is there any way to do that?"

There was. Go the length of these fences that back the parking lots facing on Mission, and he would come to a wide blacktop area between the end of the fences and the bus drive-through. See it? Well, where all them not-in-service buses are stored, just take a left down there between them buses. Take you right out to Mission.

As they talked, Rowlands also talked, almost desperately, into his phone a dozen yards away at the end of the building, as if terrified by the fact they seemed to be pointing in his direction as they spoke with Docker.

"I tell ya it's the fucker you want! Limp an' everything . . . Fuck no, he's a big mean-looking bastard, I ain't gonna . . ."

Docker was coming his way, his uneven stride lengthening as he approached. Rowlands' head ducked, so he was looking at the filth and trod-out butts on the floor of the booth. A used rubber testified to the ingenuity of the sexual urge.

"Fucker's comin' right at me, I tell you, he . . . Oh!"

Docker had gone past, throwing a quick look over his shoulder at the waiting room, not even noticing the small pudgy man talking with almost desperate haste into the phone. Docker had begun nearly trotting. Rowlands let out a long breath. A drop of sweat fell from his chin.

"Yeah, okay, I'll stay with him, but I ain't going up against him, fucker looks mean as sour owl shit."

After going the length of the chest-high hurricane fence interwoven with thin redwood slatting, Docker turned abruptly down between the rows of buses toward Mission. There was a three-foot aisle between them. In the center of the rows a bus was missing, making a large opening. Docker, out of sight of Rowlands, turned bruskly into this.

Rowlands was moving at a quick nervous walk himself by this time, hands thrust in pockets, shoulders hunched against the bite still in the air despite the late-morning sunshine, an unlit cigarette stuck behind one ear. He too turned down between the parked buses.

When Rowlands reached the end of the narrow passage, where it opened out but while he was still in the aisle, Docker was on top of him. He had nowhere to go except back, and there wasn't time for that.

The hulking blond man came around the back of the bus with the attaché case at full swing, yelling. There was nothing of science in the attack, only an apparent blind fury. The hardened plastic edge of the case caught the fat little man in the upper chest. His collarbone broke with a snapping sound like a .22 cartridge.

Docker, like a man possessed and foaming obscenities, dropped the case to thud his fists into Rowlands' lower belly. Rowlands had screamed once when his collarbone had snapped. He flew back against the side of a bus under the frightful power of Docker's blows, lit on his ass and puked in his lap. Docker set his feet to kick the fallen man in the head.

"Hey!"

He was already whirling as a second voice exclaimed, "What the fuck, man!"

Still straddle-legged and with startling agility, Docker had sprung in a complete 180-degree turn so he was facing the two black baggage-handlers who had burst out of the empty bus where they had been eating sandwiches.

One of them was a big man, big as Docker, with a scar across his forehead that said he'd mixed it in the past. Docker, in a slight crouch now, pointed a thick accusing finger at him like a ref calling a foul on Nate Thurmond.

"Freeze!" he shouted.

All fury had gone from his voice and face, so the words carried a momentary authority. Behind the horn-rims his eyes were level and observant and not at all worried. The black man froze, startled.

"You kickin' the livin' shit outta this dude," objected

the second weakly. He was a smaller man, not in condition for fighting. Grey touched both his voice and his tight-kinked hair.

"He welched."

That stopped them totally. The big one rubbed his jaw with one ham-hand. The fight had gone out of his stance. "You mean you're—"

"I mean you don't want my kind of trouble."

He made a perplexed gesture. "But, man . . ."

Docker shot a quick glance at the fallen Rowlands without giving them a chance to come at him. The little rotund grifter lay sideways in his own mess, making agonized noises as he tried to get his breath back. Docker nodded to the blacks. He chuckled.

"I guess I made my point, at that. But just in case . . ."

Before either of them could move, he drove the toe of his right shoe against the side of the fallen man's face. Rowlands cried out softly, like a bird caught by a tomcat.

Docker picked up his attaché case, nodded pleasantly to the two outraged and confused Samaritans, and limped calmly between them and down the passageway toward Mission Street. Unmoving, they watched him go, the smaller one with a half-eaten sandwich still in one hand and his mouth hanging open as if for the next bite.

When Docker reached Mission he turned left, out of their sight. He began to whistle jauntily, swinging the attaché case like a kid on his way to school with a tin lunchpail.

Seven

Going past the tellers' windows from the back of the bank, where the loan payments were made and the safe deposit boxes were kept, Neil Fargo checked his long stride. He rooted in his nearly empty briefcase for his checkbook. At one of the chest-high counters he wrote out a check for pocket money, then let two other patrons go ahead so he could get a big blond teller who carried abundant, beautifully shaped muscle and flesh over her heavy Scandinavian frame. Her placid face lit up with a display of very white teeth when she saw Neil Fargo in front of her.

"First time you've been able to find my window for months," she said.

"That's because you're so popular I can never get near you."

She made a small derisive noise in her throat. She had a lovely throat, and very clear, healthy skin. She reached for his check. He put a hand over hers, imprisoned it. She looked at him with clear blue eyes. His face wore a smile that looked insincere but at least softened his features and made them slightly vulnerable.

"You going with anyone these days, Rhoda?"

"You mean you'd care, after ignoring me for—"

He shook his head almost impatiently, but didn't remove his hand. "I'm working. I might need to have slept with you last night. Possible?"

"Hair-wash night so I was alone—you'd remember that. That's probably why you've picked me." Her wholesome expression had thinned. She said in soft bitterness, "You bastard! How long *has* it been? Six months? Seven?"

"You won't have to swear to it in court, might not even get asked, but if you are asked, it'll be by cops."

She pulled her hand out from under his, carried the check away to the big square sheaf of computer printouts which told whether it would clear or not. Neil Fargo still leaned one elbow on the counter so his heavy shoulders and broad tapering back effectively shut out anyone behind him from their conversation without seeming other than casual. The polite smile remained fixed on his face.

Rhoda returned, rubber-stamped the check, counted out a twenty, two tens, and two fives from her cash drawer. Her face was once more placid, like a dust jacket for *Heidi.* She smiled brilliantly at him across the money. She was such a big girl that her eyes were only a couple of inches below his own.

"You bastard," she said again. This time there was a hint of caress in her voice.

Neil Fargo picked up the bills, nodded, smiled, backed away from the window.

"You're a love," he said.

Ten minutes later the express elevator deposited him on one of the topmost floors of the gleaming white Transamerica pyramid which thrusts its graceful spire up from the foot of Columbus Avenue. The panorama caught Neil Fargo, held him for perhaps two minutes. It was truly amazing. From the Farallone Islands thirty miles toward Hawaii to the East Bay hills which cupped Oakland and Berkeley, from the Golden Gate to San Mateo's Dumbarton Bridge twenty miles to the south. People were mites, cars beetles, Coit Tower the end of a wooden matchstick stuck upright into an insignificant mound covered with toy houses. Only the ugly dark monolith of the Bank of America headquarters, like a stake driven into the city's heart, challenged his view.

He turned from it, pushed the button beside Maxwell Stayton's office door. Stayton Industries had the entire floor. The voice of Miss Laurence came over the speaker, tart as vinegar.

"Yes?"

"Neil Fargo. By appointment."

There was a faint click, the smooth round brass knob turned under his hand and the superbly balanced oak door, twelve feet high and three inches thick and inlaid with Tanzanian ebony, swung open. He went in. He already would have been examined on the closed-circuit TV at the reception desk, which was what would have put the asperity into Miss Laurence's voice.

"Mr. Stayton expected you at ten o'clock," she informed him in her frosty B.B.C. accent.

"I was delayed."

"It is well after eleven o'clock. Have you any idea how much Mr. Stayton's time is—"

"Just push the goddam button, mate."

Miss Laurence paled. She had mousy brown hair and close-set eyes the approximate color and toughness of manganese. She also had a walker's bulbous calves, wore sensible shoes to the office, and made forty thousand a year plus stock options. When Miss Laurence had the flu, it was reflected in that quarter's corporate earnings.

Miss Laurence pushed the button. Neil Fargo touched her under the chin with a forefinger, went through the inner door with her furious expression sticking out of his back like a hurled icicle.

Maxwell Stayton's personal office was a den with the fireplace missing. The walls were of walnut panelling that was not veneer, and were covered with framed and signed photographs of sports greats, most of them from the mid-thirties. One of the pictures was of Stayton himself, wearing a Stanford football uniform and old-style leather helmet. He was cutting, high-stepping in the photo, clutching the ball fiercely in one hand and holding off an imaginary tackler with the other.

Neil Fargo paused in front of a photo of himself, also in a Stanford uniform, bare-headed, grinning at the camera. He snapped the picture with the same fingernail he had used to chuck Miss Laurence under the chin.

As if this action reminded him of the other, Maxwell Stayton demanded sourly, "Do you have to do that to her?"

"She expects me to," said Neil Fargo. He ran his hand along the bookshelves, over leather-bound volumes patinaed by age and handling. "It confirms her view of the colonies."

Stayton merely grunted. The room, not large, was made to seem even smaller by his size. Age had distended his belly, thinned and grizzled his hair, but had not ravaged him. Behind him was a beautifully-detailed model of the *Feather River,* a 600,000-ton supertanker being built for Stayton Marine in Japan. If the ecologists could be bought or mollified, it would eventually unload crude at the Farallone Islands.

"Those football pictures stir memories?" said Stayton abruptly.

Neil Fargo crossed a rug that cost as much as a Cadillac. He looked out the fourth wall, which was tinted plate glass and echoed the reception area's views of the city.

"They're hanging on your wall, not mine."

"What do you hang on your walls?"

"Scalps."

Stayton gave a short burst of heavy laughter. He had removed a Churchill-length cigar from his mouth to speak, didn't offer a hand to shake, not even after putting the cigar down in an ashtray. The ashtray was a solid four-pound clump of polished stainless steel that a sculptor had taken a swipe at to make it a work of art. Stayton sat down behind the desk.

"You're late," he charged in a different, executive voice.

Neil Fargo appeared to bear up under the assault. He sat down across the desk from Stayton and put his briefcase on the floor beside his chair. He crossed his legs while getting a cigarette started. He waved out the match, squinted at Stayton through the smoke.

"Miss Laurence said you wanted a report on the investigation to date."

Stayton made an impatient gesture with a thick-fingered hand. "Do we have to go through all that? Just tell me—"

"I have my reports right here," continued Neil Fargo ruthlessly.

Stayton reddened slightly and leaned forward to pick his cigar off the lump of stainless steel. As he did, he said, "No calls," and in the same motion tapped one of the buttons on his desk. He leaned back. "Satisfied?"

"If that thing's closed now."

"You afraid Miss Laurence might steal your techniques?"

"It's your daughter we're talking about," shrugged Neil Fargo.

"All right, damn you, you've made your point," growled Stayton. "With all the security precautions, this had damn well better be good."

"That's how you look at it. I traced your daughter down to Mexico City, down there found out—"

"You told me that a week ago." Stayton stood up behind the immense hardwood desk, walked over to the window. He looked out over the financial district of which he owned quite a lot, turning the cigar with pensive fingers. "You've got a good thing going in me, haven't you, Fargo? Whenever Roberta decides to pick up with some deadbeat, I pay you good money to find her—"

"Because she married one of them and it cost you a lot of money to pry him loose. I'm a hell of a lot cheaper than—"

"Up until now." For the first time, Stayton showed emotion. "At least I've got a grandson out of the marriage. And *he'll* be raised right, believe me."

He came back, leaned his butt against the edge of the desk. His momentary vulnerability had hardened into anger.

"Each time I pay you a fat fee—"

"And I find her."

"And it happens again."

"This time it's different. This time three weeks up in the redwoods at a fancy sanitarium isn't going to do it."

"Meaning what?" When the younger man didn't answer, he leaned forward as if taking up his position for the snap of the ball. "I've already given you a ridiculous amount of money to cut the current one loose, and I want you to explain where it's gone—"

"Money." Neil Fargo's voice overrode his. "Money isn't the question. Your daughter's graduated from the booze, old man."

"Experimenting with drugs?" He brushed it away. "We've been through that syndrome before. Pot in a crash pad with kids ten years younger than she is—"

"Heroin," said Neil Fargo.

Stayton echoed his flatness of tone. "I don't believe you."

"Hooked. Hooked hard. Now, even if I find her . . . Christ, face it, man, in a very real sense, *no*body's *ever* going to find Roberta again. She's a zombie, a hunk of shit—"

"That's enough, goddammit!"

"—a death-wish looking for someplace to jump off."
Stayton's face was contorted. "You fucking—"

"If you can't accept that, then there's no use digging
her out of whatever rathole she's been stashed in. Treat-
ment might save her—physically—but I doubt if you'd
ever get back the daughter you think you knew. So there
it is. She's been back in San Francisco for two months,
I've learned, in one of the Tenderloin fleabags. I've got
feelers out to isolate which one, but . . . Are you sure
you want her found?"

"What a stupid fucking question," said the industrialist. During all of it, the smoke going up from the cigar in
his right hand had been absolutely steady. Neil Fargo
shrugged.

"Hell, the kid's always meant more to you than your
daughter has anyway." His voice deepened. "He's a
male heir! So we find Roberta before the H kills her,
how's he going to like reading those clippings when he's
old enough to understand them?"

"The papers won't get hold of Roberta's condition."
Neil Fargo's lips curled as he delved into his briefcase
for a file folder. "Dream," he told the industrialist.

"How sure are you of your information?"

"It's solid. I paid enough for it, here and in Mexico."

"You said 'stashed.' If you mean she's being manipulated by someone, I'll destroy them, whoever they are.
Anyone responsible for Roberta's condi—"

"Roberta's responsible for Roberta's condition." Neil
Fargo's face was unrevealing, but when he moved his
hands on the polished arms of the chair, the fingertips
left smears on the wood.

Stayton's face darkened. He reached across the desk
to drop a full inch of grey ash from his cigar into the
hunk of stanless steel. "Meaning what?"

"That addiction is psychological before it's physiolog-
ical. It starts out as a symptom, not a cause."

Stayton ran a heavy-fingered hand down his heavy
visage. He seemed momentarily unsure of himself.
"You've known Roberta for years, Neil. D'you mean
me? Or Dorothy?"

"Or Mars in somebody's seventh house with Venus ascending, or the wrong dragonfly getting stuck in amber back in the Carboniferous era. Who the hell knows what operates on people?" His voice got irritated. "Who even knows what anyone else is ever really thinking?"

Stayton nodded heavily. "I see. Somebody's bought you off. I'm to get unsupported statements of Roberta's condition, vague generalities. No names, of course, nobody I can go after and—"

"You had a chauffeur three or four years ago named Kolinski." Neil Fargo's color had heightened at Stayton's charges, but he gave no other signs of having heard them. Stayton was shocked at the detective's statement.

"Alex Kolinski? You can't be serious. To suggest that Alex—"

"He's the one who hooked her. Gave her the first fix a year, fourteen months ago. That's why she was such a good girl for so long, staying off the sauce and acting like dear mommy to the brat. She disappeared four months ago because Kolinski suddenly cut off her supply and you had cut off her allowance so she couldn't buy elsewhere. Then you wait until just three weeks ago to call *me* in—"

"Kolinski doesn't have the brains to—"

"He's not a stupid man, or an unfeeling one. He never was. You knew he was sleeping with her while he worked here; why in hell didn't it ever come up any of the times you sent me out looking for her? I've known for a couple of years that Kolinski's been a small-time H pusher."

"Pulled him off her myself, once, in his room up over the garage." Stayton was abstracted; he apparently had begun to believe Neil Fargo. "You're saying he hooked her now because I threw him out then . . ."

"That wasn't why he went after her. You know how she always was. Kicks. The chauffeur . . ." He made a gesture both cruel and illustrative at the same time. It had a startlingly feminine quality, as did his voice; he was an excellent mimic. " 'Just too *heavy,* man, daddy's *chau*ffeur . . .' He planned for years, I imagine, to humiliate her. Then somebody made it financially worth-while."

Stayton missed the cue, for the moment; his thoughts were turned inward. "She took you over the jumps once, too, didn't she, Neil? I'd forgotten that. Might not have been such a bad thing at that—though Dorothy wouldn't hear of it." He shook his handsome grey head. "Women forget so damned easy! What was *I* when Dorothy married me, for Chrissake? A fucking longshoreman's kid with a football scholarship." Steel came back into his eyes. "So this fucker Kolinski hooked my daughter. We'll unhook her. Methadone treatments, Synanon—"

"Your daughter isn't chipping, for God's sake! She's hooked. You know what that means? Five cc's a pop, three times a day. If you *could* get her to quit, what you got back wouldn't be . . . Besides, why do you think Kolinski cut her supply in the first place? To get her out of your house, out in the open where she could be controlled, eventually manipulated. He didn't dream all that up by himself."

Stayton's voice tightened further. "There's someone else?"

"A Battery Street importer named Walter Hariss," said Neil Fargo. "He and Kolinski have a number of investments together. A garage in Bush Street, maybe a couple of cheap hotels in the Tenderloin."

"I never even heard of Walter Hariss. What—"

"It isn't personal with him. He's got a wife, teen-age daughter—good family man. He wants to be big. He saw potential when he learned Kolinski was still in touch with your daughter. I think he's the one suggested hooking her. He makes fifty, seventy-five gee a year, thinks he can get his hooks into the Stayton empire through Roberta to make that half a mil a year."

"I want him destroyed."

"Legitimately?" Neil Fargo shook his head. "He's a master at never doing anything that would incriminate himself personally."

"I've paid you a lot of money to get my daughter back, Fargo," said the industrialist icily. "I want her saved. I want those men destroyed."

Neil Fargo said nothing. His face was set, stubborn. He laid his file folder on the corner of the immense hardwood desk.

Stayton said, like a bidder at an art auction, "Once Roberta is back, I will need a right-hand man. He will name his own salary . . ."

He stopped because Neil Fargo had laughed out loud.

"I wouldn't fit into your operation, Max. I've got *nostalgie de la boue.*"

"A craving for the gutter? Perhaps. You're at home in it."

Neil Fargo sneered, "So's your daughter." His eyes were furious. "It took God six fucking days to create the universe, you want two men destroyed—" he snapped his fingers "—like that. Do I get Sunday off?"

Stayton swallowed whatever reply he had been going to make. He shook his head.

"This isn't getting us anywhere, Neil. Where is Roberta?"

"Some Tenderloin hotel. There's a hell of a lot of them, and she won't be under her own name. From here I'm going down to the tax assessor's office to see if Kolinski and Hariss *do* own any hotels down there, or pay the taxes on them if they aren't owners of record. If they do, that's where Roberta will be."

He pointed at the folder.

"Quite a lot of this is in there, sanitized for that repressed sexual hysteric in the outer office when she snoops your files."

Stayton didn't bother to deny it. He pushed the folder around with the tip of the opal desk-set pen. "I want those men destroyed. If they aren't . . . well, you have a great deal of my money."

Neil Fargo was on his feet, zipping his briefcase.

He said scornfully, "Destroyed! What the fuck does that mean? Ruined? Jailed? Murdered? I don't think you've got what it would take to buy me for any of those. As for threats about money—"

"I don't threaten idly, Fargo."

But the detective met, held his eyes; and it was Stayton who looked away first. They were both big men, hard men. Neil Fargo nodded.

"I should have news about Roberta, good or bad, by tonight. Will you be available if I do?"

"I can be." Seeing the look in the detective's eyes, he added, "I will be."

"Get braced for the bad, just in case."

This time Stayton offered to shake the detective's hand.

In the immense open-air lobby below the building's stubby pillar legs, Neil Fargo used a pay phone. Pamela Gardner answered on the second ring with her formula, "Neil Fargo, Investigations." When she heard his voice, she exclaimed, "Thank God you called."

"You've got a line on Docker? Great work, doll. What—"

"No Docker. Homicide called. They want you down at the Hall of Justice as soon as—"

"Who's they?"

"What? Oh." Understanding entered her voice. She had a very good phone voice, soft and extremely sensual, which did not fit either her fresh-scrubbed little-girl looks or the way her mind worked. "An Inspector Wylie."

"Son of a bitch. Vince Wylie hates my guts." He checked his watch. "Look, doll, call him back, tell him I'll be there between one and one-thirty."

"Will do."

"And no luck with Docker, huh?"

"The only Docker in the book is on Beach Street, Neil—and that's a girl. She was d.a. when I called, I'm trying to get the landlady to—"

"Forget all that. Anything from the state?"

"DMV says no driver's license, no autos registered in his name. Ma Bell says no phone, even unlisted. PG&E is still checking, but he'd probably have the sort of place where the utilities are in the landlord's name if—"

"Yeah. Look, doll, don't wast any more time on that crap. Start calling car-rental outfits. Just for the last day, two days, he'd have to show a valid driver's license from *somewhere* to get a car—Neveda or Oregon, maybe. I've put a couple of street types on him, too. They'll call you if they turn anything. Just hit the high spots from now on. We're running out of time. I'll check in after I'm through at the Hall, if I'm not in jail."

She took it literally. "Should I alert Jack Leavitt in case—"

"I don't think Wylie has enough to make us yell lawyer yet. Instead of worrying about what might happen to me, we have to find out where that goddam Docker has gotten to."

Eight

Docker stepped off the N Judah car where Sutter Street stubbed its toe on Market. All streetcars inbound for the East Bay Terminal used Market, so the fact it was a Judah car originating out in the Sunset District offered no real clue to where he'd gotten onto it.

The blond man paused on the sidewalk in front of the ritzy new Standard Oil Building like a man undecided, swinging his attaché case as his ever-active eyes surveyed street, crowds, passing autos from behind their heavy hornrims. The air smelled of sewage, and a PG&E crew had a manhole open to look for whatever had died down there.

Docker did not seem to see whatever he was looking for. Beyond the beautiful little reflecting pool where ecology freaks liked to dump motor oil and expired seagulls whenever there was an oil spill in the Bay, a long-necked steel dinosaur was eating a dead building. Docker watched as it took another bite, seizing the edge of a wall in serrated steel jaws and shaking its head angrily when the ancient brick was stubborn about peeling away from the I-beam bones. Then the wall surrendered and the dinosaur disdainfully dropped a couple of yards of it into the rubble around its caterpillared feet.

"Spare change, mister?"

Docker brought his eyes down from the building to the panhandling hippie chick. She wore washed-out jeans and somebody else's sweatshirt and no shoes, and was as anachronistic as an Edsel. Her hair was the same ash-blonde as Docker's, just about as long and worn much the same way, parted in the center and falling to her shoulders.

"Sell your watch," said Docker.

She made a disgusted face. Despite his hair length, she said, "Fuckin' straight."

Docker turned away toward First Street. As he did, the sole of his shoe came down on the girl's bare toes, hard. She yelled. One of the yellow-hatted PG&E workmen straightened up with a shocked look on his face. It wasn't a face that had a whole lot left to be afraid of.

Docker kept going. Behind him, the girl hopped up and down on her undamaged foot and yelled curses. People watched. His eyes worried and angry at the same time, the PG&E workman put a detaining hand on Docker's arm. Docker stopped. He looked at the workman as a pathologist would look at a cadaver he was about to cut up.

The workman's gaze faltered. The hand dropped away.

"That's what I thought," Docker said.

Instead of continuing on down Market to First, he cut off down a narrow blacktopped alley called Ecker Street. His uneven stride was now springier, as if the Market Street confrontation was what he had been seeking. The alley took him between crowding ancient brick walls and eventually to Mission Street. Here he turned left, to First, crossed with the light and went out First.

The half-block to Minna Street was crowded with the sort of places which are always across the street from bus terminals, and Docker seemed to be searching again. He rejected first a drugstore that tastefully displayed its condoms on the candy counter, then a short-order joint with a back room featuring a wide variety of dildoes, merkins, and battery-operated body-massagers shapped like penises. At a bar which had SALOON painted across its front in heavy ornate circus-poster letters, he turned in.

Underneath SALOON was *All Girl Bartenders!!* in smaller red letters. Inside was a standard joint tricked out western, with a pair of plastic Texas longhorns over the back bar. Only one All Girl Bartender!! was behind the stick, wearing a Stetson and boots and a vest and a plastic pistol belt with a plastic Frontier Colt ball-ammo .44 in the holster, low on the hip of her dated red hotpants.

Docker dropped a dollar in front of the rodeo-shirted nipples she pointed at him across the bar. "Bourbon," he said.

"And?"

"Huh? Oh. Put it in a glass."

"Cute."

The girl had a hawklike, predatory face and long black hair and legs like a dancer's. Docker had his shot standing at the bar, putting it down in a lump like somebody dropping a horseshoe. The girl had no time to move away before he set the empty shot-glass back on the bar. She had no other customers to move to anyway, except a pair of south of Market types taking turns trying to sell one another pieces of the Yerba Buena Center.

"I just got into town," said Docker to the girl. "I'm looking for a whore."

"What's her name?"

Docker said patiently, "You'll do. How much?"

She leaned toward him sweetly while dropping a hand on the bar so the extended forefinger pointed at the door. She said, "And it's bye, bye, baby. Now. Out."

"Anything you think is reasonable. Just a cheap fuck—"

"The owner is an ex-pro wrestler who loves to work out on guys who four-letter his waitresses. He's out in back playing with the beer kegs for exercise. If I should call him—"

"He gets a broken arm," said Docker.

Some time went by. She sighed. She said almost regretfully, in a much softer voice, "Look, mister, I'm married. Honest."

"So was my mother, it never stopped her."

He patted the girl on the cheek and went out before she could say anything further, limping very slightly because the attaché case in his right hand put added strain on that leg. The All Girl Bartender stared after him. She wet her lips thoughtfully. Then she began assiduously wiping the plank with her bar rag, an unexpected blush mantling her cheeks.

Six doors down, Docker turned in at an open-fronted amusement arcade called Fun Terminal. Four guys were feeding the pinball machines that lined the left wall and ran down that side of the building's midline. Three of them were whites; the fourth, at the machine closest to the door, was a wasted-looking black with greying hair and holes cut in his shoes to let his bunions breathe.

The right side of the Fun Terminal was filled with half-a-hundred dime and two-bit movie peep-show machines, each showing three-minute fuck films cut into thirty-second segments. Docker bought two bucks worth of quarters and fed them into the machines, switching after each quarter instead of watching any of the brutally pornographic films out. The eyepieces smelled of perfumed disinfectant. Unlike some of the other patrons, he occupied his right hand with his attaché case rather than his anatomy.

When he'd spent enough time there, Docker walked back to the change desk.

"You ought to furnish handkerchiefs," he said to the hard-faced harpy on the stool. "I almost had an accident all over the front of one of your nice machines."

"So next time wear a rubber."

Docker crossed First Street still laughing. He ignored both the mid-block crosswalk and the angry horns and squealing brakes of the cars which the light at Mission released just in time to swerve or stop to avoid hitting him.

"I declare," muttered the black man named Browne. "He's a wild man."

As soon as Docker had disappeared into the Trailways Terminal, Browne went after him. He was slower than Docker in crossing the street, more careful of traffic and using the crosswalk, so Docker was already at the ticket window when Browne came through the swinging doors.

Browne immediately slowed to an Uncle Remus shamble down the broad aisle between the orderly rows of nearly depopulated benches. He came into earshot as the ticket agent was saying, "One-way to Los Angeles? Yes, sir. The Silver Eagle leaves in just twenty-one minutes."

Docker put his money on the counter. The lean, stooped, sad-eyed black man moved up beside him to study a posted timetable. Docker said, "What gate?"

"We . . . don't have a gate," said the ticket agent somewhat defensively. "Just outside and to your left, in Natoma Street. The bus stops there. Your luggage—"

"This." Docker lifted the attaché case, then lowered it below counter-level. "I'll carry it. What time does the bus get in?"

"Well, it makes several stops. San Fernando, Glendale, Burbank, North Hol—"

"I'm glad Trailways is hiring the mentally handicapped.

I bought a ticket for Los Angeles."

"Ten-forty tonight." The ticket agent had flushed. Docker pocketed his change. "Jesus Christ. I could walk faster."

He turned away from the window. The ticket agent turned angry, now florid features at the grey-haired black man reading the schedules.

"Next," he snapped.

"Just browsin'."

"Then quit blocking the ticket window."

Browne put his face close to the agent's. Browne's eyes had yellowish bloodshot whites. "A soft voice turneth away wrath," he said in a soft voice. "And saveth a fat lip."

He followed Docker back through the terminal. The travellers scattered around the echoing, low-ceilinged room were mostly older men buried in paperbacks or newspapers. Browne's steps quickened as Docker went toward the banks of doors opening into Fremont Street, then slowed again as the quarry turned right between the rows of benches.

This led only past a two-bit shoeshine stand and a bank of storage lockers to the men's room. Browne hesitated, checked his watch, rubbed his hands together nervously. They were long, tapering dry-palmed hands that made a rustling sound against each other. Finally the black man went into the restroom also, entering the tiled facility crab-fashion as if to avoid the full force of any blow launched at him from behind the door.

Docker was nowhere near the door. Indeed, he was just feeding a dime into the slot of the furthest pay stall in the line. He went in without looking around at all as Browne headed for a urinal. Four of the twenty-one minutes before the Silver Eagle's departure had passed.

The moment Docker's stall door had clapped shut with its heavy click designed to make the patron feel his dime was well spent, Browne drifted down the line of stalls on silent feet. He stopped just short of Docker's, precisely where the overhead fluorescents had no chance of casting his shadow under Docker's door. He listened, poised.

From inside came the rustle of clothing. A pause. Then a grunt, a splash, a relieved sigh.

Browne was already moving, quickly and silently, trotting at little short of a run toward the First Street entrance and the pay phone outside it. He dropped his dime, dialled. Alex Kolinski's heavy voice came on the line.

"He's here," exclaimed Browne, "In the men's room takin' a shit!"

Before Browne was out the men's room door, however, Docker's stall had opened. The big, blond, hard-faced man had emerged fully clothed. Docker had the attaché case pinched between arm and body again to free both hands. He was drying, with a heavy wad of toilet paper, the fist he'd used to make the splash. He dropped the paper on the floor, went out of the restroom.

In the phone booth outside the far end of the blocklong terminal, Browne was saying, "Trailways Terminal on First Street is where. He—"

"He's getting a bus." Kolinski's voice made it a statement.

"Ain't I tellin' you? Los Angeles Silver Eagle, it leaves here at twelve-twenty. He—"

"He's got an attaché case with him?"

"Uh. That like a briefcase only it square-like?"

Docker had stayed against the wall, had gone out the Fremont Street door closest to the men's room and thus had not been visible from the body of the waiting room, let alone from Browne's phone booth outside in First Street. He turned right, toward Natoma Street, then right again and went along Natoma toward First Street, where the Silver Eagle would load. The bus was waiting. Docker ignored it.

"Man, I tell you he try to leave I follow him. Be like pickin' cherries off a tree—"

"*Listen,* goddam you!" cut in Kolinski angrily. "*Don't* go up against him, hang back if he doesn't get that bus. I and some men are on the way. He beat the living shit out of Rowlands over at the Greyhound station about an hour ago, acted like he might be dropping meth . . ."

Browne, whistling cheerily under his breath, headed back into the terminal. Thirteen minutes to bus departure.

Docker, who had been standing just out of sight on Natoma, went across First Street in long strides toward the open dark maw of the parking garage directly opposite. His topcoat tails flapped around his legs and the attaché case swung in asymmetrical rhythm to help with his balance.

He pulled up just inside the door with a little skip made necessary by his limp, then twisted to scan the front of the terminal building. Browne was nowhere in sight. Satisfied, he straightened his lapels, rubbed on the back of one calf the shoe-tip of the other foot which had gotten scuffed, then went away between the rows of parked cars.

This echoing passageway took him through the sprawling dim low-ceilinged garage to a series of open-air blacktop lots. These, leased to private operators by the state, followed the course of the Skyway which shook and rumbled with traffic above Docker's head.

Eventually he emerged into Howard Street between two immense concrete abutments. He was nearly two blocks from the Trailways Bus Terminal. There was no one behind him. It was 12:18, two minutes before the Silver Eagle would leave for Los Angeles without him.

Back at the terminal, Browne was staring in disbelief as the last southbound passenger boarded the big dou-ble-decker bus. The door shut with a pneumatic sound very much like phooey. Browne sprinted back into the terminal and through it toward the men's room. In his wake moved a very big man wearing a droopy mustache that made him look like an overweight Rock Hudson during the actor's mustache phase.

Browne straightened up from looking under the locked door of Docker's empty stall with shock in his face. As he did, Kolinski came in, preceded by the over-weight Rock Hudson and followed by another man equally as large. All three of them had their hands in their overcoat pockets. No one else was in the restroom. The last man stopped and leaned against the door so anyone trying to open it would find it unyielding unless they got back and took a run at it.

Browne was backing up. Unfortunately for him, he was already at the last stall, almost against the back wall. Kolinski's deep-set eyes were dangerous.

"So?" he said.

Browne said: "I swear he . . . I come in here after I seen he wasn't on the bus. I swear—"

"Blaney?"

"He wasn't on the bus," said Rock Hudson.

"Any other bus out of here he could have caught?"

"No."

"I swear," said Browne. "I swear, Mr. Kolinski . . ."

"Daggert. Amtrack?"

"The last train out was at nine o'clock," said the man who was making sure there would continue to be no one else in the restroom.

"I swear, Mr. Kolinski—"

"Upstairs? An East Bay bus?"

Blaney merely shook his head. "He must of smelled our friend here and just split. Unless . . ."

"Yes," said Kolinski. "Unless."

Browne had gone silent. Silence did not attract attention. But Kolinski's attention was apparently already attracted. Since silence hadn't worked, Browne began trying to make himself fit into the corner formed by the final stall and the back wall. He was too long and lean and suddenly dolorous to be successful.

Then Kolinski smiled. A lot of Jews wearing tattooed numbers would have recognized the quality of that smile. "How much did he pay you to lose him?" asked Kolinski softly.

Browne's face glistened. His lips were dry. He said, "Mr. Kolinski, I swear—"

"Blaney."

The search was swift, thorough, professional, not at all gentle. Blaney shook his head. "Not enough to buy a piece of ass off his mother."

"Pure stupidity, then."

Kolinski swung a round-house right as he spoke. It was a sucker punch, but it drove Browne's head sideways against the wall tiles because Browne had made no attempt to block it, counter it, or move his head out of its way. Like silence, it didn't work either to deflect Kolinski's anger.

"Make this stupid nigger hurt," Kolinski said.

Browne's mumbled, incoherent pleadings rose to a sharp scream of pain as the strongarm's feet and hands got busy before Daggert even had time to let Kolinski out through the guarded door.

Nine

"Your cigarettes," the jump-suited guard explained to the woman in the red coat.

"But I—"

"The foil on the pack."

Neil Fargo followed her across the very slightly raised wooden ramp as his left hand gave topcoat, car keys, cigarettes, and pocket knife to the other, older guard. The buzzer sounded.

"What the hell, you packing your piece, man?" demanded the young black guard who had been hassling with the red-coated woman about her cigarettes.

Neil Fargo shook his head, stepped back, then through again. The machine buzzed again.

"Better do it," said the black.

Neil Fargo held his empty hands away from his sides, arms wide to facilitate the white guard's body search. It was sufficiently professional to seem perfunctory. The guard straightened up. Bending had made him red in the face. Small strips of his light blue shirt showed through the gaps between the buttons of his tan uniform jacket.

"My money clip," said Neil Fargo abruptly. "I always forget the damned thing."

The guard nodded and puffed out a breath laden with recent lunch. He slapped the heavy swell of gut under his jacket.

"Neil, how the hell you stay in the shape you do?"

"Night work, Ben."

Neil Fargo crossed the marble lobby of the Hall of Justice, past the bronze plaque commemorating San Francisco's police dead. The number of recent additions to the roster was one reason everyone entering the Hall was subject to a body search. He crossed to the banks of elevators at the rear of the lobby. Several professional freaks in their prescribed hippie uniforms were protesting something to a uniformed deputy who looked as if his patience was getting as thin as his hair.

The elevator was crowded with attorneys, identifiable by their attaché cases, bushy sideburns, overlong hair, and trendy clothing. The clients and plainclothes cops were drab by comparison. Neil Fargo got off at three.

It was 1:01 when he pushed open the hall door identified as the Homicide Squad. He ignored the empty reception desk and the waiting room chairs, instead went directly through the metal gate in the hip-high railing. Through a doorway was the big room where the homicide detectives lived. For years they had been only one squad of the General Works Detail, but a briskly rising murder rate, most of it connected with drug-buy burns and thrill-kills during grocery store rip-offs, had earned the squad separate quarters.

By the water cooler, Vince Wylie was arguing Brodie versus Spurrier with a huge toothpick-chewing, shirt-sleeved man whose tie had been loosened with such enthusiasm that the shapeless lump of knot was down at his third button. Neil Fargo caught Wylie's eye, then jerked his head at one of the glass-walled interrogation cubicles lining the room, at the same time raising his eyebrows.

Wylie nodded. Neil Fargo went into the room, sat down in one of the chrome and black plastic chairs which flanked the desk, lit a cigarette, drifted smoke.

Three minutes later Wylie sauntered in, followed by the cop with whom he had been second-guessing Dick Nolan's quarterback strategies. This second man was big enough to make even Neil Fargo look delicate, with heavy soft sloping shoulders and the start of a paunch under his pastel shirt. In his hip holster was a non-reg Python .357 magnum, the one with the four-inch barrel. His slacks were wrinkled like an elephant's ass from accommodating his wide butt and heavy thighs. He had eyes like Santa Claus and hands to tie bowknots in pokers.

"Should I have brought my lawyer?" asked Neil Fargo, unsmiling.

He neither stood up nor offered his hand, nor did Wylie offer his. Instead, Wylie sat down behind the desk. The big cop leaned against the edge of it. Wylie got out a cigarette and indicated the big cop with it.

"Charlie?" He made a deprecating gesture. "He's got a few minutes waiting for a witness to show up, he thought he'd sit in to—"

"Read me my rights or get him to fuck out of here."

A slow flush, the color of old bricks, rose up Wylie's heavy throat. The big cop, who had settled back with his arms crossed on his chest like a farmer settling in to discuss the weather, slowly uncrossed his arms and came erect. He took his toothpick out of his mouth, looked at it regretfully, dropped it in the wastebasket.

"They always put peppermint in them," he complained. He winked at Neil Fargo, said, "Pleasure," and shambled out.

Wylie flopped a lined yellow legal-size pad on the desk and took out a ballpoint pen as if he were mad at it. Unlike Charlie, he was wearing the jacket of his suit even though it was stuffy in the cubicle.

"Just what the hell did that accomplish, Fargo?"

"I'm going to talk in front of two Homicide cops at the Hall of Justice when I don't know what it's about? Go on with you."

"*Don't* you know what it's about?"

Neil Fargo said nothing.

Wylie sighed and lit the cigarette he had laid aside earlier while getting his pad and pen ready. The private detective watched him. Wylie laid down the just-lit cigarette without having drawn on it, and picked up the pen again.

"Bryant Street have any significance for you, Fargo?"

Neil Fargo shook his head.

"You know a man named Julio Marquez?" the silent denial was repeated. "T. E. Addison?" Again negative. "Docker?"

A light gleamed for a brief instant behind Neil Fargo's eyes. He said, "Animal, vegetable, or mineral?"

"Goddammit, Fargo—"

Neil Fargo stood up, smeared out his cigarette and put an open palm on the desk and leaned across it toward Wylie in one smooth motion. His face was tight. "Charge me with something and talk to my lawyer, or tell me what the fuck you're after."

Wylie who had also sprung to his feet as if he thought he was about to be assaulted, slowly sat down again. This time he shortened his cigarette with a long greedy drag. He stubbed it out.

"Trying to quit the goddam things, I'm down to one pack a day from three. Will power. How about the seventeen-hundred block of Bryant. *That* mean anything to you?"

"Sure." Neil Fargo also relaxed back into his chair. "Seventeen-forty-eight. I rented the upper flat there two weeks ago."

"That's good. A realtor named Deming already told us that."

"Deming's a lush."

Wylie's eyes and voice had become elaborately casual. "Ever been inside the flat?"

"Sure. When I rented it."

"That's good. Your fingerprints were all over the place."

"Who got it there?"

"Who said—"

Neil Fargo made a disgusted gesture that encompassed where they were. Wylie hesitated, then gunned sourly like Before in a Pepto-Bismol ad.

"Mex name of Julio Marquez."

"Who I already haven't heard of."

"You said that, didn't you?" Wylie stood up and put his hands in his pockets. He moved around on his feet, made clinking noises with his pocket change. A child started bawling in one of the cubicles across the room. A torrent of Spanish followed, three voices, two of them male. The voices made no impression on the child's crying. Wylie stopped moving, said, "Why'd you rent the apartment?"

"Stash a witness."

"Who? What's he a witness to?"

Neil Fargo shook his head regretfully. His chin was stubborn again. "Not unless you can tie him in to whatever happened to this Marquez. It isn't anybody named Addison or Docker and he didn't witness any murders and he isn't due in town until the end of the week anyway."

"Where were you this morning, Fargo? Between, say, five and seven?"

"Five, getting laid. Seven, trying to get it up again."

"You can prove that?"

"It's hard to get laid by yourself."

Wylie gave his hard abrupt laugh. "Boys in Vice tell me these days you can get a life-size plastic mannekin that does everything but tell you she didn't know it could ever be like that. What's the girl's name? Address?"

"Cup size?" Neil Fargo said savagely. Then he hesitated, shrugged. "Rhoda Wahlström—that's got the umlaut over the o. We use her place, twenty-one eighty-six Filbert, apartment seven. Don't talk to her at work, okay? She's a good lay and I'm not tired of her yet and she works at a bank where they'd still use quill pens if they could get the work out with 'em."

Wylie was writing on his pad. "You bachelors." He added, without looking up, "Got something on your conscience, Fargo, you're being so awful goddam cooperative all of a sudden?"

"I figure if I kiss your ass hard enough I might find out what's going on."

Wylie grunted. He laid down his pen again, made an automatic motion toward the pack of cigarettes on the desk, then with a quick, almost guilty look in Neil Fargo's direction changed the movement to sweep the offending pack into the desk drawer. He started talking in the flat impersonal voice of a trained observer used to summarizing facts.

"Anonymous phone call at seven-thirty this morning, reporting a gunshot and sounds of a struggle coming from seventeen-forty-eight Bryant, top flat. Prowl car responded at seven-forty-one, intercepted a Mex junkie named Rosas just leaving the apartment. They held him, of course, checked upstairs and found this Julio Marquez, dead. A Colt .38 auto, one shot fired. A second man named T. E. Addison in the hall—"

"Which one was shot?"

"Neither. The bullet went into the ceiling. Marquez pulled the trigger, his prints were all over the gun. Addison had been clipped on the chin and knocked cold."

"The Mex kid coked up?"

Wylie leaned back in his chair and chuckled. In telling his story he apparently had momentarily forgotten his antipathy to Neil Fargo. "That's a funny one. Just got the doc's report on him, he's a heroin addict but had shot himself a twenty-mill ampule of speed in the apartment. Said he found it in the medicine chest."

"If he's hooked on H—"

"I find out from Narco that lots of A.D.'s will use meth when they can't get heroin—apparently it helps kill the withdrawal pains. There was a second ampule of speed busted on the bathroom floor, but Rosas says that was there when he got there. That suggest anything to you?"

"That whoever killed Marquez and laid down Addison might have been high on methedrine. What has Addison told you?"

"His lawyer's phone number. Period. We ran him through R&I, all we got is that he's a chemist for a drugstore down on Market Street. He's clean, but . . . a chemist."

"Yeah. Any other fingerprints except mine in the flat?"

Wylie shrugged niggardly. "You know."

Something in his voice made Neil Fargo lean forward, face taut.

"How about glove smudges? Overlaying some of my fingerprints, maybe?"

"Yeah," Wylie admitted sourly, after a marked pause.

"Any of mine overlaying anybody else's?"

Wylie shrugged. He seemed suddenly abashed. "Deming's. The realtor's."

"Beautiful!" Neil Fargo's face wore a sardonic grin

that seemed to have genuine amusement in it. He said without heat, "You fucking bastard, you haul my ass up here—"

"You rented the place," said the homicide inspector stubbornly. "It wasn't busted into—whoever got there first this morning used a key."

"Sure. And I got one key—*one*—from Deming when I rented it, and none of the locks have been changed. What about this Docker you mentioned? Where does he fit in?"

"His name's on the mailbox." He shot a sharp look at the private investigator. "He ring bells with you?"

Neil Fargo's eyes had changed. Something glinted in them.

"What do you have on him?"

"Big cat, big or bigger than you, long blond hair to the shoulders, hornrim glasses, slight limp—"

"Deep cleft in the middle of his chin, like Cary Grant," said Neil Fargo in a very fast, very excited voice. "Spatulate fingers, excessively thick earlobes, mole up high on the left buttock—"

Wylie slapped the desk in delight. "You *do* know him. All right, goddammit, now I *will* read you your rights. You have . . ."

His voice ran down. Neil Fargo had given one short, vicious burst of triumphant laughter, then had gotten very busy lighting another cigarette. The brick color rose sharply up the back of Wylie's neck again. His fingers flexed as if seeking a nightstick around which to curve. Neil Fargo met his eyes lazily through the drifting smoke.

"Docker," he said in a thoughtful voice. He shook his head in a parody of regretfulness. "Never heard of him."

Wylie was silent for nearly a minute. The flush receded. He had been shooting judicious looks at Neil Fargo's pack of Pall Malls. He succumbed and reached across the table and speared one. When he spoke, only the thinnest edge of his bottled rage touched his voice.

"All right. Call it square."

"You said the name was on the mailbox. Couldn't he just be a former tenant?"

"Could be." Wylie's voice was soothing as cough syrup now. "Maybe, when you rented the place, you saw his name already on the mailbox and just forgot it? Maybe you just left the old nametag on there?"

In flat, indifferent tones, Neil Fargo began. "Maybe. I didn't look at the mailbox, I knew I wasn't going to get any mail there, all I want the place for is this witness who has a thing about hotels . . ." He suddenly chuckled. "What happened, the lab boys tell you that nametag on the mailbox was brand new? And you hoped I'd say I saw it there two weeks ago?"

Vince Wylie's silence was eloquent. He lit the cigarette he had bummed. Neil Fargo went on without heat.

"How do you tie that description you gave me to the name Docker? The realtor?"

"You dealt with him, Fargo. It ain't long enough between drinks for his records to be anything but a handful of flea dirt."

"Then who gave you the description? Addison? Marquez, speaking from the dead?"

Wylie's voice was almost ashamed. "Rosas."

"The *hype?*" Neil Fargo started to laugh. "Jesus *Christ,* Vince, you ever hear the one about Little Red Riding Hood and—"

"All right, all right, but the guy's story was goddam rational. He was waiting around for a new pusher to show up in Franklin Square, his other connection got busted—"

"Did he?"

"Narco confirms a collar there yesterday. Anyway, Rosas says this big blond guy with the limp we think is Docker comes out of seventeen-forty-eight around seven-thirty this morning. Rosas is desperate for a fix, he thinks this cat might be the new connection, so he follows him. This guy makes him, knocks him around a little, acting high himself, you follow me? Erratic, paranoid, hyperactive."

"Speed freak?" mused Neil Fargo.

"Then the blond guy tells Rosas there's a dead guy and an unconscious guy in this flat that he can rob, and some speed in the medicine chest he can sell for smack, and the key's in the mailbox and good luck."

Neil Fargo nodded. "And then this Docker—if there is a Docker—calls the police himself in hopes Rosas will be blamed for Marquez." He looked keenly at the Homicide cop. "Awfully talkative hype, isn't he, this Rosas? What do the people in the downstairs flat say?"

"It's empty."

Neil Fargo stood up, smeared out his cigarette. The flat Indian planes of his face were carefully devoid of emotion.

"You take a name off a mailbox and tie it in with some big blond guy nobody's seen but a heroin addict who's strung out to the point he'd sell you his left nut for a fix, and you have the guts to haul my ass down here—"

"You rented the apartment," repeated Wylie stubbornly.

"That don't mean I killed anybody in it. You got two live ones besides this—maybe—Docker at the scene, why pick on me?"

"Addison? Rosas?" Wylie shook his head. "No way. You ain't got the picture, Fargo. Marquez got knocked right over the couch. *Over* it, friend. From behind. Got his neck broke landing on the floor. That looks great on TV, but it takes one fuck of a lot of raw power to really do it."

Neil Fargo had his topcoat back on, was standing wide-legged in front of the desk like a captain on the bridge unconsciously braced against the roll of his vessel.

"When can I get my apartment back? I'm still gonna have a witness to stash, no matter who got knocked off where."

An almost triumphant look came into Wylie's pale cop's eyes. He said, "It's got a police seal on the door, so maybe you better leave your key with me for the time being." He paused expectantly.

"I don't carry it around with me, for Chrissake."

Wylie's face lit up; he opened his mouth.

Neil Fargo said, "Call my secretary, tell her to drop it in the mail, you want it so fucking bad."

He stopped there, laughed again when he saw how sullen Wylie's face had gotten.

"The key in the mailbox. You hoped I'd given it to Docker." He stared at Wylie, then shook his head in apparent disbelief. He said, "Cops. Jesus Christ."

Wylie stared after the tall, lithe figure until Neil Fargo had passed out of the squad room. Then he sighed and shook his own head, and fished a cigarette out of the pack he had put in the desk drawer.

"Shit," he said aloud to no one in particular.

Down in the lobby, Neil Fargo stopped at the cigarette counter for another pack of Pall Malls, even though he had opened the one in his pocket just before entering the Hall of Justice. As the blind man behind the counter waited on other customers, Neil Fargo chatted with him. Then, when they were momentarily alone, Fargo leaned closer and talked earnestly in a low voice. He seemed to be explaining something and the blind man seemed to be memorizing several things.

"I won't let you down, Mr. Fargo."

"That's the boy, Jimmy."

Before leaving the Hall, he used a phone booth to get Pamela Gardner. She said she was eating a sandwich at her desk. She said she was working through the car-rental outfits but she'd had no luck so far. None of Neil Fargo's informants on the search for Docker had called in. Docker himself had not called in. Then she had a practical question of her own.

"Did you talk with Maxwell Stayton?"

"Yes, doll. No fires burning there. I'm on my way to the assessor's office now to keep you from jumping down my throat tonight."

Her relief showed in her voice. "So we won't need Jack Leavitt after all."

"Nope. Still out of the slammer. But that reminds me. You'll find an apartment key in the left corner of my middle desk drawer. Mail it off to Vince Wylie at Homicide, will you? I want to piss him off. And I want you to dummy up the Dahlberg file so it looks as if we're expecting Eric LaValley up from L.A. next weekend as a possible surprise witness. Can do?"

"Sure. But Neil . . ."

His chuckle was soothing, as if to allay the anxiety which had reappeared in her voice. "Just getting at Wylie, doll. Really."

Ten

The office at 858 Bush Street was just large enough for a steel safe as squat as a hydrant, a table, a desk, three straight-backed chairs splattered with the paint of ancient refurbishments, and a bottled water dispenser. The single door opened on the garage floor. Beside it was a tall square inset table with a stool in front of it. The table was just large enough for a time-punch machine and a cumbersome antique cash register loaded with silvery curliques.

The office itself smelled of oil and gasoline and dampness and old socks. Walter Hariss was behind the desk; with his pearl-grey hand-stitched suit and two-dollar cigars he was as incongruous as Spode in Woolworth's.

"*Missed* him?" he demanded. Anger reddened his firm round face.

"We kept the fucker in the city," grunted Kolinski.

"All he has to do is rent a car—"

"No driver's license, according to Fargo."

Hariss shrugged meaty shoulders under expensive tailoring. Restless, he stood, went to the door, peered out into the garage. He could see the dark polished length of his Cadillac, with the top of Gus Rizzato's head showing behind the steering wheel.

"*Steal* a car, then?" he suggested.

"And drive it where?"

Hariss turned back. His expensive arm waved to indicate the wide world. Kolinski shook his head emphatically.

"Can you think of anywhere more vulnerable, once somebody's got a make on you, than behind the wheel of an automobile on a freeway?" A rare sunny smile twitched his lips. His arms came up holding an imaginary machinegun. He sprayed the room with it as his mouth said, "Phtoo-phtoo-phtoo-phtoo-phtoo-phtoo-phtoo," then added *"Fwoom!"* His eyes watched the car rolling and burning.

"We don't have the manpower to cover all four freeways out of this city," objected Hariss.

"Docker doesn't know that."

"And if we did spot him—what about our dope? What about the hundred-seventy-five gee?"

"Docker can't take the chance that we *won't* cut him down."

"Then what *will* he do? You know a fugitive's psychology better than I do, this is a new—"

"You're a fucking delicate flower, I know. He'll hole up. Head for an airport. Rent a private plane . . ."

"Fargo said he's got all the small airfields in the bay area covered."

"You trust that fucker." It was said in a tone of amazed disbelief.

"Did I say I trusted him?"

Hariss might have elaborated on his methods of safeguard against Neil Fargo's possible perfidy, but a woman had come to the door with a ticket in her hand. Kolinski looked past her, saw the door of the restroom shut and the light on, so took her ticket himself and ran it through the time-punch. His deceptively Neanderthal features were pleasant.

"Ninety-five cents, ma'am," he beamed.

He gave her back her nickel and handed the ticket to the only car-park attendant who was on the floor during the slack midday hours, and who had just emerged from the john. He was a black-haired kid with a wiseass face, wearing a white jacket grimy around the cuffs and creased across the seat from sliding in and out of cars. He went off to the vertical manlift to the upper floor where her car was stashed.

The woman wandered vaguely toward the cigarette machine. After staring thoughtfully at her back for a moment, Kolinski went back into the office.

"Nice ass on that broad."

"We're out a quarter of a mil in heroin, and you're staring at women's backsides." Hariss' voice was filled with distaste at the wanton vulgarity.

"A woman's ass might find us Docker if he's holed up in town."

Hariss listened intently as the angular bony man told him what Robin had come up with concerning Docker and his sexual habits. Listening, Hariss could not stay still: he perched on the corner of the desk, sat behind it, stood, fidgeted, cracked his knuckles all together with a swift palms-out shoving motion of both interlaced hands.

"How sure are you of Robin?" he asked finally.

"She didn't make it up, if that's what you mean. She supplied details about Docker himself."

The woman with the nice ass got into her Saab and left. The dark-haired boy headed for the candy machine beside the office door.

"I meant, how sure are you that she won't get the information and then hold out on you?"

Kolinski's eyes gleamed as if with remembered lust. "No way. I own that bitch."

"I hope so," said Hariss equably. "Remember, I am playing for much higher stakes in this than a kilo of heroin. Roberta Stayton is my entrée to her father's commercial empire."

"I've told you before and I say it again, Walt, that old bastard is nobody to mess with. I worked for him—"

"I didn't," said Hariss drily. "Through your persistence and vindictive nature, we . . . possess Stayton's daughter. He does not yet know this. Once he does, he will not know who I am until I have been legally granted . . . certain rights in Stayton Industries."

"He knows who I am." Kolinski's voice was glum. "All he has to do is see me." He suddenly slammed a frustrated fist into his open palm, and his voice became a rant. "Goddam that fucking Docker! It was all so easy, right now we should be counting hundred-dollar bills . . ."

"Do you really think Docker planned this alone?"

"There isn't anybody else."

"There's Neil Fargo." His heavy features were judicial; he looked like a man who would make laws rather than break them. His eyes became suddenly murderous without a muscle changing in his face. "If Fargo *is* mixed up in this hijack . . ."

"He ain't been breaking his ass to shower us with information, has he?" Kolinski checked his watch. "*One* phone call, to say Docker doesn't have a car or driver's license—and it's goddam near two o'clock . . ."

Hariss nodded, a somewhat worried look on his face. He drummed thoughtful fingers on the desktop. The dark-haired youth started into the office, munching his candy bar, checked at whatever he saw in their faces or sensed in the room's atmosphere, and went away hurriedly.

A look that could almost have been fear flitted across the grey-haired importer's heavy features.

"There's something else, Alex."

"About Fargo?"

"About Docker. A . . . pattern of erratic behavior that . . . that's worrisome. We have assumed that Docker, realizing the exchange point between the money and the heroin was our weakest spot because we worked through agents rather than being there ourselves, decided to take *both* the money and the heroin. Correct?"

"Correct," said Kolinski.

"Then let us follow his actions for the last six hours. Before Addison arrives, he attacks and kills Marquez. He now has what he supposedly wants. Does he leave? No. He waits for Addison, knocks him cold—but does not kill him also. Why?"

"Leaving him for a fall guy for the Marquez murder," said Kolinski promptly.

"He needed no fall guy *until he was seen.* Nobody except Neil Fargo, up to that point, knew what he looked like. Now Addison does. Then he goes into Franklin Square, talks with a junkie there, and sends *him* up to the flat also. Then, almost assuredly, he phones a tip to the police about the dead body in the flat."

"Setting up *another* possible fall guy."

"Except Addison is still alive to testify the junkie *isn't* the killer."

He paused to light a cigar, turning it evenly in the flame of his lighter. He talked around the rolled, saliva-wet leaf, then used it as a pointer to jab home his points.

"See what I mean by worrisome? It makes no rational sense. He acts as if he is high on something himself. Supporting this theory, my police informant has told me that there was a broken ampule of speed on the bathroom floor."

"Did you ask Fargo if Docker is hooked on anything?"

"When he first mentioned Docker, he said he'd been a North Vietnamese POW for a couple of years. He might have gotten habituated to painkillers subsequently in a military hospital. But that's academic; this isn't: does Docker attempt to leave San Francisco?"

"He does," said Kolinski. "First at Greyhound—"

"Does he? At Greyhound he acts like a man out of control, attacking Rowlands with the utmost ferocity. Then he coolly convinces two witnesses he is a Mafia enforcer. Later, he shows up on Market Street and makes himself very conspicuous in an encounter with a hippie panhandler. He makes himself obnoxious in a First Street bar. He makes flip remarks in a peep-show emporium—"

"As if he *wants* to be spotted," muttered Kolinski. For the first time, his face reflected some of the concern apparent in Hariss' voice.

"Exactly. Incredible stupidity, one would say at first glance. After all, he has what he wanted: the heroin and the money which was to be used to buy it. Why attract attention?"

Kolinski said haltingly, thinking it through, "But then

when he *is* spotted, he pulls some sort of very cool switch to disappear completely and leave us running around in circles . . ."

"As if he's laughing at us," said Hariss. "Why? Is he indeed erratic, or is he playing some sort of game? And where is he? And why hasn't Neil Fargo come up with anything further—"

The phone rang.

Kolinski picked it up, spoke his name into it, listened. He cupped the receiver with his hand and turned to Hariss. "Neil Fargo. He's got news about Docker."

Eleven

Walter Hariss moved with a fluid grace surprising in a man of his obviously self-indulgent habits, plucked the receiver off the wall phone over the squatty safe in time to hear Neil Fargo's voice demand sharply, "Who else just came on besides you, Kolinski?"

"Hariss," said the fleshy importer.

"Good. Half an hour ago Docker rented a car at a joint down the other side of Market. It's a canary yellow Montego, this year's or maybe last year's model, two-door sedan—"

"License?" Kolinski's pen was poised.

"No got. My man spotted him walking out on Howard, lost him when he ducked into a second-hand office furniture supply warehouse in the eight-hundred block. Twenty minutes later, my man made him again, just driving the Montego out of the car-rental outfit. He wasn't in close enough to get the license—"

"Why in fuck didn't you tell him to go in and get it from the girl behind the desk?" snarled Kolinski.

Neil Fargo's voice instantly hardened. "Listen, asshole, I'm getting this all relayed through my secretary. I wasn't in touch with this guy direct. I'm not sitting around my fucking office waiting for Docker to come in and sit in my lap."

"What's the name of the rental outfit?" asked Hariss soothingly.

"Never mind that, I'm on my way down there now. I'll let you know when I pick anything up."

Kolinski began, "Listen, goddammit—"

He stopped. He and Hariss were listening to the empty buzz of a dial tone. Hariss slammed a hand in frustration against the dirty plaster wall of the office. His face was very pale.

"Who does he think he is?" he panted. "Get Gus."

Kolinski leaned out the door to bawl across the garage at the diminutive chauffeur. "Gus! Get your ass in here."

Rizzato immediately popped out of the Cadillac, trotted up to the office. He should have been comic in the long dark blue coat and peaked cap he affected while behind the wheel of the limousine, but no figure of fun ever wore eyes like Rizzato's.

"Yessir, Mr. Hariss?" He stood in the office door like a dog waiting to be told which way to point. Hariss laid the hand which bore the cigar on his narrow muscular shoulder.

"Gus, I want you to go over to Neil Fargo's office. There are some things I want you to find out."

Obscure excitement sparked the little man's eyes. "I'll ask that secretary of his."

"With restraint, Gus. With restraint. For now."

"Yessir, Mr. Hariss."

"All right, three things. When Neil Fargo came into his office this morning was he carrying a package? A newspaper-wrapped package, perhaps? Two, is there such a package at his office now? Three, did a call actually relay information about Docker renting a car, and was a license number mentioned which the secretary passed on to Fargo? Now, on your way." He let the diminutive chauffeur get to the door before calling after him, "Restraint, Gus. For the moment."

Hariss sat down again half-smiling; his good humor was quite restored. He drew on the cigar, put his head back to drift the rich smoke at the ceiling.

"I don't get it," said Kolinski. "What's with this package? And what's with Gus and Fargo's secretary? Shit, she's a fucking kid, nineteen, twenty years old."

Hariss said in a measured, distasteful voice, "She excites him."

"Yeah, well, she's small enough for him at that. Probably the only broad in town he could let get on top without—"

"Alex, if our association ever terminates, it will be on the basis of your verbal vulgarity—"

"Yeah, I know, Walt—but you don't mind taking your cut out of the FarJon Hotel operations."

"Business is business. All right: I sent Gus over to Neil Fargo's office to make sure the missing hundred-seventy-five gee's aren't hidden there."

"You mean the paper-wrapped package—"

"Of course. We have only Neil Fargo's word for it that Docker ever *had* that money. Assume for the moment that he and Docker, at least initially, planned the hijack together. Docker's attaché case could have been taken to the Bryant Street flat *empty,* merely to serve as a receptacle for the key of heroin."

"Yeah!" exclaimed Kolinski softly. "I like that." His expression changed. "But Fargo's not stupid. He wouldn't leave the money in his goddam office. He'd put it in a safe deposit box or—"

"Events have moved rapidly. Docker may have betrayed Fargo as well as us. Safe deposit boxes cannot be reached until ten A.M., he may have had to leave the money in his office and may not have had a chance to collect it since. In any event, the girl will know whether he brought a package, a briefcase, anything which could have held the money into the office with him this morning. And Gus will make sure there is no money there now."

Kolinski's eyes had sharpened again. "And checking up on whether the information about Docker's car-rental came through the secretary—"

"Fargo may have held back a license number, let us say, that would aid your people materially in spotting Docker's car."

"But why would Fargo—"

"Alex, I'm surprised at you." He laid aside his cigar to illustrate his words with gestures. "Let us turn it around and suppose that Fargo is *not* involved in the hijack with Docker. That means that *somewhere* out there is a man with a hundred-seventy-five thousand dollars in cash, plus heroin worth a quarter of a million on the street once it has been cut to the standard five percent." He chuckled. "Fargo may very well feel—as we do— that if he could beat the other principals to Docker—"

"I see." Kolinski's bony face had become pensive. "But if Fargo's stringing us along, he'll have briefed his secretary on what to tell us."

Hariss chuckled richly. "Gus has an extremely persuasive way of asking questions of young ladies."

The back of Gus Rizzato's open hand drove Pamela Gardner's delicately-boned skull sideways against the plasterboard partition beside her desk. The pigskin driving gloves he wore left a mottled red pattern on her cheek.

"I asked you about a package, dearie."

Outrage and terror fought in the girl's face. In a voice high with fear but still defiant, she exclaimed, "You, you . . . get out of here! When Neil hears—"

The knuckles whipped across her cheek the other way. She broke, screamed, scrambled from her chair so she could get the desk between them. Rizzato's dainty size six shoe swept sideways against her ankles, slamming them together and taking her feet out from under her.

Pamela went down heavily on her side, only partially breaking the fall with one hand. In the same motion she tried to roll under the desk in a flurry of nyloned thighs.

Rizzato's hand darted down between the churning legs. The girl screamed again, whether in pain, further terror or outrage was impossible to distinguish. She kicked up and out; her shoe missed Rizzato's face by the slimmest of margins. Since she was on her back she used elbows, bottom and heels to scrabble backward into the well under the desk like a threatened spider into a corner.

Rizzato was around the desk as quick as a weasel. He grabbed her short brown hair from behind as she emerged, jerked her head up and then back and sideways to rap it just hard enough on the edge of the well. The girl made a strangled sound in her throat as if she were trying to retch. He rapped again. The girl quit fighting his hands.

"That's it, dearie," he chirped. His eyes and voice were cheerfully birdlike. He bent his own face over hers, so he could look down into her fear-haunted eyes. "Now tell me about the package."

"There wasn't any—"

Rizzato reached down his free hand and almost contemptuously massaged one of the small ripe globes beneath her fuzzy yellow sweater. The girl's body stiffened, her mouth opened as if in rictus, but she made no sound.

Rizzato removed his hand. Blood congested his face, either from rage or arousal. "Answer my questions, dearie, or I'll strip that sweater off you and suck on that nipple until it's the size of a grape. Now out from under the desk and on your feet, no tricks. Right?"

There was a long pause. Pamela finally nodded her head, mutely. Her face was nauseated. A thin line of blood had run down one corner of her mouth where she had bitten herself.

"That's my girl. Now tell me about the package."

Rizzato stepped back three swift paces, stood poised on the balls of his feet as she awkwardly crawled out from under the desk. The girl was shivering as if with cold. She shot a single shamefaced look at Rizzato, then looked at the stairwell.

"I locked the downstairs door, dearie. Neil Fargo, Investigations is closed temporarily for inventory."

"If Neil should come back—"

"He's out looking for Docker."

The girl shuddered. She pressed back against the edge of the desk. Her body shielded her right hand from Rizzato's view. The hand crept back, spiderlike, toward the telephone.

Rizzato had removed his suitcoat, carefully hung it over the back of a chair. To go with his six-inch-wide necktie, he wore bright golden suspenders three inches wide. Somehow, these did not make him look ridiculous.

He reached back as if to scratch the back of his head, then his arm was a sudden blur and a slim black commando's knife was lying on his open palm. The girl's hand leaped back to her side as if scalded. Rizzato laughed complacently.

"Fargo must have told you why they call me Peeler."

The girl made her eyes find his face. Her pupils had dilated with emotion like a cat's, so almost no iris showed. Somehow she made her voice low and steady.

"You don't have to hurt me. I'll tell you anything you want to know."

"That's my girl. Did Fargo bring a package with him when he came in this morning?"

"Package?"

"Dearie . . ." He pointed the flat black blade at the front of her dust-marked skirt. "Maybe I'll open you up down there so you can take a stallion right to the balls and yell for more."

The girl's face became exactly the shade of parchment. It took her lips, so dry had they become, three times to whisper, "Please . . . I . . . don't know what you mean. He . . . was empty-handed. Completely."

"There's this morning's *Chronicle* on top of the file cabinet."

"I brought that myself. I bring it every morning."

"Now we find out if you're lying."

The office was small, with few hiding places. Only one filing cabinet was locked, and that one Rizzato dumped on its face and opened by working loose the lock-rod. There was no package, no money. Finally he heaped up some of the dozens of file folders he had dumped out, unplugged the coffee pot, carefully removed the basket which held the sodden grounds and dumped them over the files. He completed the destruction by pouring the steaming coffee over the grounds. Then he sat down on the edge of the girl's desk.

"And now, dearie, tell me about this car Docker is driving . . ."

He left exactly twenty-two minutes after he had first entered the building. Since the Bush Street garage was less than eight blocks distant, he drove directly there to report in person. Then he went back out to sit behind the wheel of the Cadillac again.

Inside the office, Hariss said, "So. Fargo is clean so far as we can determine. No money, no package—"

"And an informant actually did call in with the information Fargo passed on to us about Docker's rental car. And he passed *all* of the information on to us."

"We may have been unduly suspicious of friend Fargo."

Kolinski blew air through his nose. "Unless he called the info in to her himself."

"She would have recognized his voice."

"She could lie—"

"To Gus?"

Kolinski was silent for a moment. Then he nodded. "*I* wouldn't want that little bastard coming after me." He chuckled. "I wonder what Fargo's reaction is going to be when he sees his office."

"Gus can take care of himself."

"Against Fargo? I watched him play with the Forty-Niners." His voice was suddenly worried. "I hope that bastard never finds out that we've got Roberta Stayton stashed in the Tenderloin while he's running all over hell looking for her."

"I would say we have much more proximate concerns that Neil Fargo," said Hariss stiffly.

As if to punctuate his remark, the telephone rang. It was 2:47 P.M.

Twelve

At 2:24 P.M., Docker had gone up the stairs of a faded residence hotel midway along the 600 block of Geary Street. It was a neighborhood of cheap bars, buildings torn down to make way for parking lots, and beyond mid-block, post-quake construction totally without charm.

The heavy varnished front door, its glass protected by twisted wrought iron rods, was open. The way Docker entered made it apparent that he had known the door was unlocked. He limped down the hall on a cheap carpet given spurious depth by the foam rubber pad beneath it, went through another door at the far end of what once had been a quite ornate lobby. A mirror gave him back his own bulky image fragmented by the silver peeling from the back of the mirror.

Rough concrete steps led down a half-flight to another door. This was old, weathered even on the inside, painted a faded yellow which looked almost brown in the dim light. The light over the door didn't work. Docker let himself out.

This put him in a low-roofed, concrete passageway. At the far end was scraggly foliage, ground-hugging juniper and a wildly out-of-place Fatsia japonica, whose deeply indented spatulate leaves were turning brown from lack of chemicals in the soil. Down a dozen groaning wooden stairs was a narrow alley.

Docker turned left, went along the littered blacktop to pause in a doorway on the right-hand side with his back against the door. The building was of faded red brick. The doorway had a red EXIT light above it in a metal cage. Docker drew on his cigarette, let his eyes roam behind their hornrims. No one was in sight.

Docker ground out the cigarette against the wall, pocketed the stub, pushed backwards against the door. It opened with his weight, he slid through. He was at the foot of dark narrow stairs. He went up them through the gloom, laboring a little with his right leg yet sure-footed, his fingers in their surgical rubber serving as delicate antennae to aid his orientation as do a cat's whiskers.

At the top of the stairs was a firedoor. The hand that did not hold the attaché case turned the knob. This door was also unlocked. Docker opened it a scant inch, laid an eye to the strip, saw only empty hallway with peeling grey walls and a grey threadbare rug with a pink flower design like spilled animal guts.

He let the firedoor click shut behind him, crossed the hall in two quick strides, twisted the closest knob, went through the door and shut it behind him.

The junkie whore called Robin had turned around the chair over which Kolinski's coat had earlier been thrown to face the room's lone window. This stared out at a red brick airshaft through greyed nylon curtains. The open window let air stir her lank hair and the greyed curtains. At this hour oblique sunlight touched only the upper third of the age-softened brick wall opposite.

Robin smiled at Docker over her shoulder, thus throwing her head back and tightening the muscles in her neck to give her throat a smooth deceptive grace. Her face was pinched; normally, she already would have used the second of the glassine bags of heroin Kolinski had left with her.

She laughed softly at the expression on Docker's face. There might have been the faintest note of hysteria in her merriment. If Docker noticed, he let nothing show in the smile he found to put on.

"He brought your name up himself this morning," she said. "I didn't have to maneuver him at all." Docker said nothing. She said, "I can't ever get used to . . ." She stopped, shook her head. She said, "Have you got it?"

Docker opened the attaché case on the bed. "I've got it." He held up one of the baggies of pure heroin for her to see, tossed it on the rumpled covers. He delved again, and dropped on the blanket beside the heroin a ten-cc syringe that looked the twin of the one which Kolinski had used on Robin that morning. "You?"

"In the top drawer of the dresser."

Docker sighed. He sat down on the edge of the bed, legs thrust wide in front of him. He stared glumly at the cracked dirty linoleum. His position was so unconsciously reminiscent of Kolinski's that morning and all the other mornings that the girl shuddered.

"Is this the way the world ends?" she asked softly.

Docker raised his head very quickly to surprise the momentary horror on her face. She was still sitting in her chair, knees drawn up to her chest, arms locked around her folded legs. Only her bare feet showed beneath the frayed hem of the nightgown.

"We don't have to go through with it, Robin."

"Daphne's going to call at two-forty-five. You saved out the five thousand?"

"Yes."

Her eyes were suddenly feverish with rage. "He hurt her this morning. He loves to hurt people. He calls her Aunt Jemima."

Docker sighed again. "Robin, I still think . . ."

She ran a hand through her hair. There was some of that morning's urgency back in her movements, but it was under control. The dregs of the dose Kolinski had administered still remained in her body. The sweats and sniffles were still some way off.

"I thought about getting my hair done," she said. "Putting on makeup, buying a robe. Then I realized that would ruin it."

Docker took a turn around the room. His face was icy behind the glasses; a faint sheen of sweat had appeared on his forehead. He didn't meet her eyes. He looked at his inexorable watch as at a bomb. He stopped by the sink, leaned over it as if he wanted to vomit into it. He straightened, turned, leaned back against the wall. He seemed disinclined or unable to stand up straight; being on his feet seemed to tire him.

"Yes," he said harshly. "Business as usual for it to go down. But . . ."

"The time for 'buts' is gone." She paused, added his name deliberately, almost mockingly, as if tasting the shape of it with her mouth. "Docker. The time for anything is gone. Time is gone."

"It doesn't have to be—"

"For me it does."

She stood up, crossed the linoleum on bare narrow feet. Her skin was luminously pale. Although she was a tall woman, her head fit under Docker's stubborn chin. The chin was already lightly stubbled since his morning shave. She reached up, removed his glasses, folded them, stuck them end-down in the outer breast pocket of his jacket.

She said against his chest, "Jesus, I'll be glad." She leaned back to look up into his face, then pressed hers against his chest again. "You understand that, don't you? I'm tired, tired in my soul."

Docker put a hand wedge-shaped with muscle under her chin, tipped her head back, bent and with a ritual tenderness pressed his open mouth against hers. It was a long, sexually alive kiss, though the lips of both man and woman were dry and feverish. Her arms went around him, clung fiercely.

She broke the kiss so she could whisper into his mouth. "I wondered whether I would wish we'd saved time for it. Now I'm glad we didn't." She suddenly giggled. "I'm probably syphed up again."

"Robin, there's still time to call it off . . ."

She didn't bother to reject his plea. She began softly humming a dance tune. To a few bars of it they actually danced, a dream-like waltz step from a long time before. Docker's limp was not apparent in their slow matched movements. They were graceful together.

"Remember?"

Docker nodded. "Twelve, thirteen years ago. The grand ballroom of the St. Francis."

She stopped dancing.

"Miss Stayton was the hit of the Cotillion. She was stunning in her cerement and shroud."

"For God's sake, Robin—"

"Twelve, thirteen centuries ago, baby. I'm old. Ancient. Burned out. Time?"

Before he could check, she twisted his thick wrist so they could read his watch together.

"Two-thirty-three," she said.

She walked away from him without a tremor of hesitation, pulled open the dresser drawer which contained her treasures. She set aside the handkerchief-wrapped syringe very gingerly, as if it were fragile crystal. Then she quickly and efficiently arranged her matches, her candle, her bent tablespoon. These defined her physical world, these were her Shakespeare folio, her Gauguin original, her Hope Diamond.

Without being bidden, Docker got the baggie of heroin and the syringe from the bed. He set the attaché case on the floor.

Robin heaped the tablespoon three-fourths full of the terrific jolt of white powder. She added water at the sink, returned to move it gently over the candle flame. As she worked, she talked, her voice almost sprightly, snatches of poetry, the Shakespeare line about motive and cue for passion.

In a suddenly flat rational tone, she demanded, "How pure?"

"Ninety-five percent."

A shiver ran through her, whether from anticipation or fear or merely from bare feet on cold linoleum was impossible to tell. She tipped up the spoon, filled the opened ten-cc syringe.

"The hottest shot in the world. The ultimate flash. My usual is five percent." Her eyes glittered. She was sweating badly, pouring sweat; great moons of dampness had appeared under the arms of the flannel nightgown.

"Be by me, darling," she said.

She sat down on the edge of the bed, holding the hypo in her left hand as her right delicately began working to bring up the veins. She was so totally absorbed in this that it was obvious her absorption was spurious, or rather was intensified so as to shut out all other thought.

Docker had no such anaesthesia. Sweat poured off him to equal hers. In a hoarse voice he said, "Robin . . ."

She shook her head. Her tongue came out one corner of her mouth in concentration. She switched the syringe to her right hand, then, with the suddenness of a fisherman gaffing a shark, she rammed the needle into her arm.

"Got it, first try!" she exclaimed.

She did not yet depress the plunger. She laid back on the balled-up pillow and looked at Docker almost joyfully. In her movements had been none of the hesitation which had seduced Kolinski into injecting her that morning.

"Two months I pretended to dislike the needle. A lot of hypes really do, you know." She met his eyes almost mockingly. "Darling, I'd do it if you were here or not. Accept that. The only difference is that it'd be wasted." She drew a deep breath. "Time?"

Docker had been sidling closer. Unthinking, concealed desperation glinted in his eyes. He turned the action of checking his watch into a sudden lunge for the syringe. His hand was still a dozen inches from it when her thumb rammed the plunger home. Her body arched slightly.

"Are you in such a hurry for me to . . . oh! Oh, Jesus Christ! It's beautiful! It's pure . . . pure . . ."

Her face now wore a look of utter ecstasy. Her hand was already relaxing on the syringe. Her feet were drooping outward as the muscles of her calves and ankles relaxed.

"So . . . so sleepy-tired!"

"Robin. Oh, Jesus, Robin . . ."

Her face was relaxing, smoothing out. Her eyes under suddenly sleepy lids were now very clear. The angles of her face were elegant and fine and altogether lovely.

"Shleepy," she said gaily. "Sh-h-h . . ." She raised her head with an effort. "I don't love you, you know, darling. Not anymore. We just . . . You . . ." She stopped as if she would not be able to speak again. Then she said in an abrupt clear surprised voice, "Who would have believed it'd all . . . all shlip . . . all . . . away . . ."

Her head rolled sideways on the pillow. Her right hand fell laxly away from the hypo, so it flopped over against her arm, the neede still sticking in her vein and raising a long narrow ugly blue-looking welt of flesh with its imbedded length. Her breathing was regular but already growing shallow.

Docker stared down at her with a shocked look on his face, as if he could not believe the speed with which the deadly infusion was working. In a tight, agonized voice, he said, "Jesus, oh, Jesus, Robin, what have we . . . Wasn't there any . . ."

His voice died away. There was no response, no movement from the girl on the bed. Her breathing had lengthened further, was becoming labored. At that instant the needle, responding to gravity and its own weight, slid from her arm. It fell past the edge of the bed.

Docker moved with dazzling speed, his hand shooting down and out and snapping shut around it just as it touched the floor. It had no chance to break. He straightened slowly with it clutched in his gloved fingers. He was breathing heavily. His eyes looked as if he wanted to scream. Yet by catching the hypo before it could smash on the floor he seemed to have made his ultimate acceptance.

For some minutes he stood unmoving above her, watching her chest continue to stir under the faded flannel. He stooped, laid a hand on her ribs, pressed delicately up under the meager flaccid globe of her left breast.

"Presque morte," he said in soft sorrow. The two isolated French words had a finality that their English equivalents lacked. Nearly dead. He seemed to be searching for the hard edge of that finality.

Docker drew a deep breath that was also a sob, came erect, then bent once more to touch his lips to hers. They were warm and yielding, as if she were dropping into sleep instead of death.

He said, "Goodbye, Robin."

He crossed quickly to the dresser, picked up the handkerchief and its burden the way he would have picked up a primed charge of *plastique*. He held it beside her left elbow, then let the handkerchief drop open so the syringe fell on the floor where the other would have struck if he had not intercepted it.

Docker stepped back, regarded the scene critically, then carefully toed the syringe a little further under the bed where it would not be instantly apparent to anyone entering the room. He was working with fine tolerances now.

Docker opened his attaché case without lifting it from the floor, put in the hypo which had killed her, withdrew a banded sheaf of bills. They were hundreds, fifty of them. His gloved fingers laid them on the corner of the dresser.

One last quick look around the room.

Breeze gently stirring the dirty lace curtains, very slightly guttering the candle on the dresser top. Sunlight gone from the mellowed brick wall opposite. Spoon. Ripped baggie which had brought her the death she sought.

He looked at his watch. He touched nothing except his attaché case and the doorknob going out. He left the room, the building, by the same route he had entered, like a cloud passing from the pale face of the moon. The goose-plump black girl using the pay phone at the far end of the hall did not see him go. No one saw him go.

It was 2:47 P.M.

Thirteen

Elided syllables made the voice on the phone as rich as chicken gumbo.

"Mist' Kolinski, you gotta come over here right quick—"

"What? Who the hell—"

"This here's Daphne. At the hotel? It's Miss Robin. Mist' Kolinski, she . . ." The voice paused, became suddenly intimate with puzzlement or dread. "He was *here!* Dat man. Dat man who *limps.* He was in her room, I seen him . . ."

Kolinski's hand mauled the receiver as if it were Docker's neck. Kolinski's own voice sounded strangled.

"Is . . . he *still* there?"

"He surely isn't. But when I seen him go by de desk, I went down to Miss Robin's room 'cause I was scared . . . I mean, Mist' Kolinski, she was askin' me 'bout whether I know which girl was with him las' week, an' . . ." Her voice quavered with terror at his possible displeasure. "An' Mist' Kolinski, it was *Miss Robin* he was with last week!"

"You fucking black bitch, what are you telling me?" His voice snapped Hariss erect, alert.

"She's . . ." The Dixie voice got even closer to the phone, so it had the intimacy of intercourse to Kolinski's ear. "She's done shot herse'f up, Mist' Kolinski! She's already goin' on the nod, an' she *laughin'*. She sayin' you gonna have to wait for her to come down off her high 'fore she tell you where he's at. An' she say you gonna have to beg her . . ."

"You fucking cunt!" Kolinski screamed at her.

He slammed down the receiver, twisted toward the door. Hariss was in his way. Hariss put a small beautifully-groomed hand on his chest. It stopped Kolinski like a log through the windshield.

"Get hold of yourself."

"Docker was just up at that fucking Robin's room! The nigger cunt spotted him sneaking out, and . . ." He was fighting for control and ramming his arms into his overcoat. ". . . and after he left, that fucking bitch shot herself up."

"And?" Hariss' voice was ominous.

"Robin told the spade she knew where he had gone but that I was going to have to crawl to get the information."

Hariss quoted drily, " 'I own her.' You ignorant, strutting animal! You . . ." He stopped, shook his head almost in admiration. "Strong genes. Her father's daughter . . ."

Kolinski was once more at the door. "What pisses me, Walt, I left her those two extra bindles of shit this morning myself. So she could use them to . . ." Flecks of spittle had appeared at the corners of his mouth. His eyes were quite mad. His hands convulsed themselves like dogs fucking. "She figures because she'll be on the nod before I get there—"

"Alex."

"I'll get her awake and I'll—"

"*Alex!*" The importer's tone slashed through his rage. Kolinski tried to meet the other's eyes, couldn't.

He growled, "Goddammit, Walt, I—"

"Crawl for her, Alex, if that is what is necessary."

Kolinski drew a deep breath. His rage was passing. He nodded. "Yeah. Okay. Whatever I have to do to find out where he is. But afterwards . . ."

"Of course. Afterwards." As Kolinski started for the door, Hariss added, "One further point."

"Christ, Walt, I gotta—"

"The point is that Docker has a car. Yet he pauses to confer with a junkie whore with whom he casually slept a few nights before."

"Well?"

"Why hasn't he gotten out of town?"

The two men stared at one another with a recognition dawning between them. Mixed in with the struggling comprehension were the first hints of personal fear. It was Hariss who voiced it.

"Docker?" he whispered. "And Robin? And what does he want?"

Kolinski blustered, "When I get through with that bitch, we'll have a lot of answers."

His voice was that of a boy drawing a line in the dirt and daring a bigger boy to step over it. The lights of the small office raised a sheen of perspiration on Walter Hariss' heavy features.

At the same moment Kolinski stormed out, Docker lowered the wrist with the watch on it so he could look through the smeary front window of the narrow pensioner's hotel directly across from 517 Jones. That was the address of the second-floor hotel in which Robin Stayton had just completed her dying.

Docker dropped a dime, dialled. His eyes were intense behind their hornrims, his lips were pursed almost as if he were counting. The pay phone was isolated in the front corner of the lobby, well away from the old men watching the afternoon soaps on the lobby TV. By merely switching his gaze downhill through the smeared window, to the coffee shop on the far corner of the O'Farrell Street intersection, he could see his quarry.

In the front booth were a red-haired man and a black-haired man, the redhead in profile and the other with his back to the window.

The phone was ringing. Docker was chewing on a wad of toilet paper. Through the window he could see the coffee shop's Chinese waitress reach under the counter to pick up the receiver.

"There should be two men sitting in the window booth drinking coffee," said Docker, as if he were not where he could see them himself. His voice labored like an asthmatic's around the wad of moist paper. "One of them should be a red-headed Irishman—"

"Say, who is this? What do you—"

"The other should be a Jap. Tell the Jap he's got a phone call."

He watched the waitress pause, decide, lay the receiver against her breast so he could no longer hear her breathing or her voice as she leaned across the counter. Her mouth moved. The back of Henry Tekawa's sleek black head jerked to her words. He stood swiftly, went to the counter and put one knee on a deserted stool so he could lean forward to take the receiver.

"Tekawa," he said.

"Docker again."

Tekawa had a voice as smooth as butter, totally unaccented. He was third-generation American. He said, "Mr. Docker, my partner and I have wasted almost forty-five minutes drinking lousy coffee in a crummy cafe because—"

"Shut up!" The viciousness in Docker's voice came

through the wad of paper. Quasi-hysteria joined it there. "You fucking cops are always the same! Lean on everybody, always lean on people! Only now I'm doing the leaning. I hang up this fucking phone and you're fucked, Tekawa. Got that?"

"I could hardly miss it." Tekawa's voice was light, almost humorous. He turned and scanned the street casually through the window, took in the enormously fat man in a light-colored sport coat who was wedged into the public phone booth on the other side of O'Farrell. "You called me yesterday, Docker, said—"

"I'm doing the talking," cried Docker. Tension whined in his voice. He too could see the fat man in the phone booth. He paused, so when the fat man gestured again he could speak in rhythm with the gesture. "I'm offering you a big bust, Tekawa, and you come on cop-heavy with me . . ."

"A drug bust, I believe you said yesterday?"

"It's bigger than that today."

Tekawa moved his eyes to his redheaded partner and back to the fat man in the phone booth. As he did, an aging queer with a slack mouth and avid eyes and dandruff on the shoulders of his black ribbed sweater came out of the liquor store a few steps from the fat man's phone booth.

"Bigger?" prompted Tekawa.

"Murder," said Docker.

His mouth smiled around the disfiguring wad of paper as he saw the redheaded narc start very casually across O'Farrell with the green light, sauntering toward the fat man. Just as he reached the curb, the fat man hung up.

Tekawa said very quickly, as the redhead looked questioningly back at him, "What do you mean, murder?"

"Quit stalling me, man," snapped Docker. He slid a thin blade of paranoia into his voice. "You tryna keep me talking, is that it? You tryna keep me on the line so you can trace the call? You tryna—"

"From a phone I didn't know you were going to call me on?" Tekawa shook his head at his redheaded partner, who stood on the curb facing downhill, which put his back to Docker. His hands were in his pockets; he teetered on his toes, idly. Tekawa went on, "Hell, Docker, you sound like you've been around long enough to know it's damned near impossible to make a trace with all the electronic equipment they use today anyway."

"Yeah. Sure." Docker's voice was mollified. "I'm strung out, that's all."

"Strung out?"

"There you go, fucking leaning on me again!" he cried. He said in more rational tones, "Just an expression, that's all."

He stopped there, waited. He watched the fat man unwedging himself from the phone booth. The fat man was fat enough so his belt must have been a sixty; his shoes, chronically asked to support a weight no shoes could long support, were run over so far that the outside edges of the uppers were worn through.

The fruiter took the fat man's arm tenderly, as he might have taken a woman's. Both Docker and Tekawa were silent, both watching the little domestic drama. The fat man had taken the paper-wrapped bottle from the fruiter's other hand like an infant reaching for a breast. They moved away together.

Docker, in his window, mouthed silent syllables into his phone in case Tekawa could see him through the glass despite the reflections from the street. Tekawa finally broke the silence.

"When you say murder, Mr. Docker . . ."

"Murder One."

Kolinski, hands thrust into the pockets of his expensive coat, lean as a mortician, was turning into the street door of the FarJon Hotel across the street. His face was set and grim.

Docker said excitedly, "He's giving her an overdose."

"Who? Where?"

From his coffee shop, Tekawa could not see the door up Jones Street that Kolinski had just entered. His partner, who was staring down Jones toward Market, had his back to the door.

"You ever heard of a man named Kolinski?"

"I may have." Tekawa's voice had become instantly

guarded. Docker was watching the second sweep of his watch now.

"Don't be so fucking cute, Jap. Your nuts ache you want him so bad. So he's just given her an O.D. It's a deliberate hotshot—ninety-five percent pure shit."

"Nobody has pure—"

"This came out of a hijacked shipment where a courier from Mexico got wiped this morning out on Bryant Street. Wylie's on it from Homicide."

In tones he attempted to make casual, Tekawa began, "I may have heard something—"

"Kolinski's going to split if you don't get up there."

Tekawa's cool finally slipped. "Where, then, goddam you?"

"Five-one-seven Jones. The FarJon Hotel. Get up there, Jap. You'll hear the coon on the desk screaming when you go through the street door."

Docker depressed the hooks but kept talking into the dead phone. He also turned slightly so his shoulder and part of his back were to the window to make him seem unaware of what was going on in the street outside. Past the black plastic edge of the phone he watched Tekawa burst from the coffee shop and cross O'Farrell against the red light. The redhead fell in beside him; they went up Jones in strides so long as to be nearly running.

They tried the narrow dirty street door of the hotel, found it locked, mashed the buzzer.

The door opened.

Something, perhaps something they heard, made them start drawing their pieces as they went in and then out of sight up the stairwell.

Docker grimaced around the wad of mushy paper, released the hooks of the phone, dropped another dime as his eyes stayed on the gaping doorway of the FarJon Hotel. He dialled. When Pamela Gardner's voice spoke Neil Fargo's name in his ear, followed by the formula Investigations, he said, "Roberta Stayton. FarJon Hotel, five-one-seven Jones."

Docker hung up on the girl's repeated demands to know who was calling. Something in her voice made him stand frowning for a few moments before melting away through the lobby, to a side door which let him into an alley which in mid-block intersected another alley which finally let him out into the 500 block of Geary. That was where he had left his rented canary yellow Montego. His dime's worth of meter had not run out during the time it had taken Robin to die.

Fourteen

Neil Fargo waited for the traffic to pass before jay-walking across Franklin Street from the Seventy-Six station on the corner of Pine. Behind him, Emil called in his heavy Hungarian accent, "Dammit, Fargo, what you think? You think rent a stall entitles you—"

Neil Fargo, on the far side of Franklin, paused to wave back at him as if at a good joke, went on. His long legs covered ground rapidly without any semblance of hurry. At Bush he turned three doors uphill to his office, which was upstairs over a laundromat, and a beauty shop managed by an Oriental woman with whom he had slept several times and who ran a small book on Bay Meadows and Golden Gate Fields in season.

When he started to open the street door to his office, it didn't open. His thumb reflexed twice against the latch before the message got through. He stepped back two paces and a snub-nose .38 appeared in his right fist. The fist was sufficiently large to make the gun look as if it were made out of licorice. He obviously had not been wearing it when he had been frisked at the Hall of Justice some two hours before, which meant he had left it in his Ford Fairlane before entering the cops' domain.

Now he thumbed back the hammer as his left hand sorted out the office key, inserted it, turned it delicately. The lock was well oiled, so Neil Fargo was inside with no sound.

He left the door ajar behind him, went up the inside edge of the otherwise rather creaky stairs, moving with a grace and silence unnerving in such a large man. His head very gradually rose above the level of the floor. This allowed him to see between the two-by-two wooden posts which supported the railing along the edge of the stairwell.

Pamela was sitting at her desk with her head in her hands. He stood there for quite thirty seconds, observing her, before she drew a deep shuddery breath and raised her head. She wiped away a tear from the corner of her eye with an oddly defiant gesture, turning her head in the process so she was facing the stairwell.

Her eyes were red and puffy, at first glance blackened horribly by a multitude of blows. The eyes widened. She threw a hand up to her mouth and screamed.

Neil Fargo was already racing up the stairs, going by her in a smooth deadly rush to smash wide the door of his office. He swung quickly, kicked open the door of the restroom so viciously that his toe splintered the wood, stepped around the cheap copy machine against the rear wall which might have sheltered a crouching figure. Still in the same motion he thrust the gun, butt forward, into its belt holster on his right hip.

The sequence had been so swift that the girl was still exclaiming, "Oh! It's you! Oh, thank God!" as the gun went back into its spring holster.

Pamela came out of her chair and into his arms as he stepped over the pile of coffee-ruined files. She was a full foot shorter than Neil Fargo, so he had to stoop to hold her. He patted her shoulder, the back of her head, crooned soft words, his voice and movements remarkably gentle. His face, over the top of her head, was absolutely murderous.

"It's okay, doll," he said in a monotone. "It's all right now, nothing more's going to happen, it's okay, doll, nothing more . . ."

She was crying again. She got out, "Oh, Neil, I'm . . . I couldn't help . . ." She curled against his chest like a kitten, looked up at him from tear-stained eyes. "I couldn't . . . He . . ."

He released her, squeezed her shoulder warmly with one hand while pulling her down into her chair with the other. He clattered down the stairs to slam the front door. He started back up, frowned, then turned back to twist the lock-knob so it shot home the bolt with an unmistakable thud. Then he went back upstairs.

Pamela had found her purse and mirror. Seeing him from the corner of her eye, she even found a ruefully tentative smile. She shook her head at the image of her own puffy, flushed face. The black marks under her eyes were from tear-streaked mascara, not from fists.

"Party's getting rough," observed Neil Fargo cheerfully.

"I'm sorry, I couldn't . . . When he left, I locked the door, I was afraid he'd come back . . . and I wanted to call you down at the assessor's office, but . . ."

"Afraid who'd come back? Docker?"

"*Docker?* Oh, no, it wasn't . . . It was that terrible man who drives . . . the one who . . ."

"Peeler?"

"Yes."

"He put his hands on you?"

She met his eyes, her own miserable, quickly looked away again. Neil Fargo nodded as if she had answered his question.

"He rape you?"

Shock registered in her face. She blushed. Finally she looked down at her hands flat on the desktop, fingers spread, and shook her head.

"Oh, no, Neil, he. . . . It was questions he. . . ."

The detective hooked one haunch over the corner of her desk, swung his leg from the knee in a hypnotically soothing rhythm.

"We'll do something about him, doll," he said placidly. He leaned toward her slightly. "Do you think you might be up to telling me what he wanted? What he said and did? Everything?"

Pamela told him everything, her face forlorn. She stumbled over any detail about the way Rizzato had put his hands on her. The very omissions were quite graphic. Her telling took less than three minutes.

"Before Rizzato got here, had anything more come in on Docker's car that he got? License plate or anything?"

"Oh! License plate!" she cried. Excitement momentarily displaced the revulsion on her features. "The same man who called about the car originally called back and said the license was—"

"Before Rizzato got here, or after?"

"After."

"And you bore up well enough to get the information, even after he had slammed you around? You're a wonder, doll."

The wildness, which had started to enter her eyes again, died in a flush of delight at the frank admiration in his voice. She said, "The license is 636 ZFF. Mercury Montego rented this . . . Oh!" she exclaimed suddenly, breaking in on herself.

Neil Fargo's foot stopped swinging. "What, doll?"

"Just a few minutes ago, another call! A man spoke Roberta Stayton's name, and then gave me an address—"

Neil Fargo banged his fist lightly on the desk in glee. *"That's* the way, doll!"

"She . . . The address was on Jones Street . . ." She was rummaging paper on her desk. "I think it's a Tenderloin hotel . . ."

Neil Fargo had gotten rigid. He said softly, "Five-one-seven Jones?"

She had found her paper. "Five-one . . ." Her face fell. "How did . . . ?"

"The FarJon Hotel," he said bitterly. "I just found out at the tax assessor's office that Alex Kolinski and Walter Hariss are owners of record and also pay the taxes on the FarJon Hotel at five-one-seven Jones. We're breaking our butts looking for Roberta Stayton, and those . . ." He stopped over the word he had been going to use. "And they have her at their fingertips."

"Ha—have?"

"She's hooked, doll. On H. Hooked hard."

"You didn't put it in any of the reports." She looked almost hurt.

"Verbal only, direct to Stayton. That's what I was telling him this morning. His executive secretary snoops all his files, so I didn't want to put it on paper." His eyes had gotten thoughtful. "The FarJon! I know the place, a real dump, equal proportions of whores and old farts you have to move from chair to chair with a shovel. If I'd known those mothers had her *there* . . ." He stood up briskly. "Well."

He pointed at the telephone.

"Call yourself a taxi, doll, go home. I'll lock up when I leave."

"Neil, I'm all right. Really. I—"

"Home with you, doll. Have your mother give you a glass of sherry or something." He frowned abruptly. "The informant who called, did he identify himself?"

The girl got a surprised expression through her tears.

"Neil, it . . . it was . . . it was that man! Dock-er."

"Docker?"

"I know it's silly, but I . . . really, I told you, he has this mushy voice like . . . like loose teeth. I . . . it was the same voice as this morning! I'm sure it was."

Neil Fargo started to say something, then merely leaned down and took her dainty pointed chin in one huge paw, squeezed it gently.

"Call yourself a taxi, doll, put in an expense voucher for it. I'll wait until the cab gets here. I've got some thinking to do anyway." His face was set and cold. He added, almost to himself, "About just how much else I don't know."

"Neil . . ."

But he had turned and gone into his private office and had sat down behind the desk. He left the door open but his action had discouraged further talk. Five minutes later the taxi honked below the window. He went back into the outer office. Pamela was pulling on her coat. She made a hopeless gesture at the room.

"I should clean up this mess . . ."

"I'll have the janitorial service do it," said the detective.

At the head of the stairs she paused hesitantly again. "Neil, shouldn't . . . shouldn't somebody call Mr.

Stayton and tell him we think we've located his daughter?"

"I have to make sure she's there first, doll. Besides, you don't know that old bastard. He'd be down there trying to get the hotel condemned or something. This is going to take handling. You go on home."

As soon as the outer door had shut behind the girl, Neil Fargo went directly to her phone, picked up, dialled. He drummed impatient fingers on the desktop through two rings.

"Hariss? I just dropped by my office. Pam tells me that your driver was around to ask a few questions."

Surprise smoothly entered the importer's voice. "Gus? Gus wouldn't go off on his own like that, Neil."

"I know."

"Well, now you mention it . . ." Sly laughter danced around the edges of his words. "Yes, I guess I did tell him to drop around at that. Wanted him to ask your secretary where you might be reached. You've been pretty hard to get hold of today."

"I thought we had a business arrangement," said the detective in curiously flat tones. The laughter abruptly went out of Hariss' voice.

"We do, Fargo. *Do,* not did. You try to back out—"

"Since we have a business arrangement there's nothing I can do about you at the moment, Walt. But sometime along the line I'm going to be wondering why Roberta Stayton happens to be living in a hotel that you own, with me knowing nothing about it even though you know I've been hired by her old man to find her. But—"

"Now, Neil, there's a reason—"

"But even that can wait. This can't. I want you to go out and tell that little cocksucker you call a chauffeur that he doesn't work for you anymore."

"What?"

"That he doesn't work for you and that his ass is going to be out of San Francisco by tomorrow morning."

"That's the most ridiculous—"

"Because if I see him after tonight, Hariss, see him on the street, see him in your office, see him *anywhere,* just lay eyes on him, ever, I'm going to kill him. You got that?"

"If you think—"

"I mean dead, Hariss." The very flatness of his voice lent absolute conviction to the words. "He put his slimy fucking hands on my secretary. Not busted ribs, not a broken arm, not a ruptured kidney. Dead. Dead and buried. I'll be in touch."

He slammed the receiver down on the hooks. He was breathing deeply and harshly. His hands were shaking. Almost immediately the phone began ringing. He stood, pulled back on his topcoat, walked out of the office and away from the ringing phone without even looking at it. He locked the office, went back across Franklin Street to the Seventy-Six station where he parked his Fairlane.

He maneuvered the metallic blue car out of the slot in which it had been buried, just as Emil slapped a calloused, grease-rimed hand against the fender. Neil Fargo stuck his head out of the open window.

"I'm in a hurry, Emil."

"Fargo, what you do now?" He waved an arm at his precious parking slots as if Neil Fargo had not spoken. "What I do the man who rents the stall shows up, huh?"

Neil Fargo made a suggestion concerning Emil and the car which belonged to Doctor Follmer, the stallholder, that was quite impossible even though the doctor's car was a compact. Emil was still cursing the detective in his broken English when the blue Fairlane drove off. The garageman stared after him with bushy eyebrows drawn down angrily. Then he gave a sudden laugh, and shook his head fondly.

"One crazy bastard," he said in admiration.

Fifteen

San Francisco's Tenderloin has changed for the worse over the years. For several decades it was merely tough and a little raunchy: now it is nasty as well, like perfume behind the ears of a corpse. Seedy hotels with Rates for Senior Citizens still cater to the aged, but now the old folks living on inflation-ruined pensions must rub shoulders and mingle life-styles with whores, topless dancers, pushers and users, cool black cats, teen-age male prostitutes, transvestites looking for sailors.

Coffee shops feature Breakfast All Day; bars turn on their garish neons at six A.M. Violence is endemic: drifting hard-eyed men roll drunks and gays and the fragile aged and cripples, both emotional and physical, as a way of life. Hustlers and grifters con social workers getting their jollies from seeing Life in the Raw, and one day at a time is how people live. Because in the Tenderloin anything can happen and sooner or later everything does.

Certainly the girl who panhandled Neil Fargo as he got out of his Fairlane was just hanging on by the hour. She would have been attractive if she hadn't had lice and smelled bad. She was under twenty, wearing blue wash pants and a blue sweater and a crust of dried vomit around her mouth.

She asked for spare change as if for salvation. He gave her a dollar bill. She smiled shyly at him.

"You want a nooner, mister . . ."

He shook his head, watched her shamble up Jones Street. He shook his head again, finished locking the Fairlane, fed the meter, and started across the street to the FarJon Hotel.

In mid-stride he swerved downhill. A black-and-white was parked in the bus zone with one door hanging open and the radio crackling. He went into the liquor store on the corner, stood with his back to the door in deep contemplation of a quart of Early Times. A paddy wagon with mesh over the rear windows pulled up in the yellow zone on O'Farrell with a squeal of worn brake linings.

In a little more than two minutes, a pair of uniformed patrolmen went by the open door of the liquor store. Between them, wearing handcuffs and a dazed expression, was Alex Kolinski. He was having a little trouble with his feet. There was a trickle of blood down his chin and above the right eye a hard red knob which looked shiny. The cops looked tough, competent, and untouched.

Neil Fargo laughed aloud, catching the attention of the liquor store clerk. Men with stimulant-blown minds who chuckled and whistled and smirked to themselves before going berserk would be no rarity to him. The cool competence in Neil Fargo's face seemed to reassure him.

The wagon had pulled out with its prisoner. Neil Fargo walked uphill on Jones with quick strides. The narrow door of 517 Jones was standing open under its faded *FarJon Hotel, Weekly Rates* sign. He went in.

The stairs were very narrow, the handrail slick from a million sliding hands. Insulation-wrapped steampipes ran up the corner of the stairwell. There were rat droppings on one of the wedge-shaped corner steps which made the ninety-degree left turn under the tilted mirror Kolinski had used that morning to watch Daphne go down these same stairs.

At the head of the stairs was another uniformed prowlie. Behind him Neil Fargo could see the office door with a hand-lettered sign over it:

NO CHECKS CASHED
RENT DUE IN ADVANCE
NO VISITORS AFTER 11:00 P.M.
EXCEPT YOU GOT YOUR OWN KEY TO LET THEM IN

The cop was holding one of the extra-long riot-control billies, the sort Tac Squads have made so popular, at present-arms across his chest. His face was too young, too unformed for his hard, competent body or for the cop's eyes experience had already given him.

"Sorry, sir, residents only." Neil Fargo moved a hand, and the face was suddenly as tough as the rest of him. His voice barked. *"Hold it!"*

"Just I.D." Neil Fargo got it out gingerly. "I had a tip that a skip I'm looking for is holed up in this dump."

The cop returned the I.D. "Sorry, sir, but we've had a homicide here."

"Homicide?" His voice was unsurprised, as if Kolinski being led away had partially prepared him for it. "Wouldn't be a woman, would it?"

The cop's eyes sharpened. "Think she's the one you're looking for?"

"Could be. First name Roberta—although she probably wouldn't be using her real name here."

"Our D.O.A. is called Robin by the manager. The Lieutenant'll want to see you." He turned to yell down the hall, "Lieutenant Tekawa, sir."

"Tekawa? What's a narc doing in charge of a homicide?"

The cop spun back to him. *"Lieutenant* Tekawa to you, Jack. And narc isn't a word we—"

"Is that Neil Fargo you got?" Tekawa had appeared in the far end of the corridor. "Come on up, Neil."

Neil Fargo went by the prowlie without saying anything; the cop's face had closed up at being bypassed. The private detective paused in the doorway of Robin's room, his eyes taking it in: the body on the bed, now with a sheet drawn over the face; the candle stub; the junkie's paraphernalia; the chair turned toward the airshaft. The sunlight had now entirely departed from the red bricks opposite.

"Seeing how the other half lives, Hank?"

"Sometimes I think I ought to transfer to Bunco." Tekawa's gesture encompassed it all, from the dirty handprints around the light switch to the overflow stain

in the corner of the ceiling above the sink. "Little old ladies conned out of their life savings might be a pleasure
instead of junkie O.D.'s. I don't think you know my
partner, Jerry Maley."

Neil Fargo and the redheaded cop shook hands. The
redhead looked like a cop; Tekawa, slim and elegant
and bland-faced behind studious glasses, looked like an
assistant professor at Cal.

"You'd get bored with the pigeon drop, Hank," said
Neil Fargo. "That how you read this? Simple overdose?"

"Take a look," invited Tekawa. "But no touchie:
Homicide and the interns haven't seen her yet."

He watched Neil Fargo raise a corner of the sheet to
look down at the dead girl's face.

"There goes a fat fee," muttered the private detective.

"Someone you know?" Curbed curiosity made the
Japanese cop's eyes sleepy and his face even more
bland. Neil Fargo let the sheet drop.

He said, "If it's an accidental overdose, how come I
see Alex Kolinski being led away in bracelets when I
come in?"

"We walked in on him," admitted Tekawa. "Black
girl on the desk was having hysterics. Had a bruise on
her jaw, and one on her tit, and said she got them from
Kolinski when she tried to follow him into this room.
Said she saw him with a hypo in his hand and the deceased on the bed before he shoved her out. Could be
lying, of course . . ."

"Kolinski's one of the owners of the building," said
Neil Fargo abstractedly, as if not really thinking about
what he was saying. "Along with Walt Hariss he pays
the black girl's salary."

"Well well well," said Tekawa softly. "Didn't know
you were interested in real estate."

Neil Fargo jerked a thumb at the bed. "In her."

"Did you notice the syringe rolled under the edge of
the bed? Beautiful set of latents on it. If they should be
Kolinski's . . ."

"It'd break your heart." Neil Fargo added in an

amused voice, "I saw you had him resisting arrest a little bit."

Maley turned from the window, where he'd been staring down the airshaft as if carefully disassociating himself from the conversation. He had pleasantly blunt Irish features, wavy red hair just being touched around the edges with grey.

"Kolinski panicked when he saw us in the doorway behind him, tried to bust out. Past Hank."

"Hai!" yipped Neil Fargo softly. He went suddenly into the karate front stance, threw in rapid succession an upward knife hand and a fisthammer, stepped away into a back stance, straightened, relaxed, laughed, and said, "Bullshit."

"Don't let him fool you," said Tekawa to his partner. "He could put a bottom fist through this wall without bruising anything but the plaster."

"I'd rather stand six feet back and throw an ash tray at 'em," grinned Maley. His voice hardened. "You said you were interested in the deceased, Fargo. Exactly what did you mean by that?"

"Whoa, hoss," said the detective softly. He looked at Tekawa. "You figure out yet why Alex Kolinski might want to O.D. a two-bit junkie whore?"

"That's what worries me," admitted Tekawa. He looked as worried as a slab of bacon. "She was going to turn him as a pusher?"

"Hank, we both know the connection isn't a son of a bitch to the hype. He's Mr. Nice with the big cotton candy."

"Accidental?"

"I don't see Alex Kolinski making in front of a couple of narcs the kind of mistake Alex Kolinski wouldn't make in the first place. If he was O.D.'ing her, it was a deliberate hotshot."

Maley had been frowning from one to the other. He stepped suddenly in front of Neil Fargo, put a hand on his chest and shoved, not hard but not gently. Neil Fargo gave back a pace. Maley repeated the action. This time Neil Fargo didn't move. Maley was nearly as tall as the private detective, but without the tremendous over-lay of muscle the ex-pro footballer carried.

"You didn't answer my question, Fargo. And we don't feel like answering yours."

"Sweet and sour, Hank? Honey and vinegar? Even to people who just see it on TV, that's a wheeze. If you want me to get into trouble just have him put his hands on me again."

"Jerry. It's okay." Henry Tekawa's soft, unaccented voice had a hidden whiplash in it.

Maley stepped back looking confused, as if he wasn't used to being denied his partner's backing, especially in the time-honored police whipsaw of one cop being nasty, the other friendly.

"Which leaves you being tipped," said Neil Fargo.

"Right," said Tekawa. "That he was not only over-dosing her, but with a hotshot of ninety-five percent pure shit. Somebody named Docker—"

"An anonymous tipster who gives you his name?" Neil Fargo started to laugh sardonically.

"He called me yesterday at the Hall, asked for me personally. Voice like he was eating mush. Very aggressive, very nervous, quick—hyper, you understand?"

"Dropping amphetamines?"

"Could be. Said yesterday he would give me a big drug bust, said he'd call again this morning. He did."

"Hank, are you sure—" Maley began.

"It's okay, Jerry," said the Japanese again. "He told us to be at the greasy spoon down on the corner at two-fifteen. We waited until two-fifty for his call. He stalled around, suddenly said Kolinski was up here killing somebody with an overdose."

"Knew ahead Kolinski was going to do it, waiting for him to show up." Neil Fargo's eyes gleamed. "Or was Kolinski maybe framed for it?"

"Not if it's his fingerprints on that syringe. And not unless somebody bought the black chick on the desk to screw down the lid on him. Christ, Neil, I'm not sure the girl was even quite dead when we came in." He paused. "Okay. Your turn."

"Buttering up your partner?" grinned Neil Fargo.

Maley's face darkened and his fists clenched at his sides, but he said nothing. His eyes were on Henry Tekawa, filled with a veiled anger and contempt.

"*You* weren't after Kolinski, were you, Neil?" asked Tekawa softly.

"No. A girl."

"*This* girl?"

"You have to ask?" His face was suddenly tired. "Voice like he was eating mush, you said. Same kind of voice called my secretary just before three o'clock, said I'd find my subject at this hotel. Didn't identify himself as anyone named Docker, but it was probably the same guy."

"And who is the subject?" Tekawa's voice was still soft.

"Her name was Roberta Stayton."

Jerry Maley, who had been silently prowling the tiny area of free floor space between the bed and the window, stopped abruptly. He let his breath hiss out between his teeth.

"As in *Maxwell* Stayton?"

"His daughter. Spoiled rich kid, the old story—debutante coming out ten or twelve years ago, when debs still came out, Stanford, then a quick marriage that cost the old man fifty thou to cut loose, a son from it. After that, pretty wild."

"You went to Stanford yourself, didn't you, Fargo?" asked Maley. There was frank insinuation in his voice.

"Yeah. And I knew Roberta Stayton there, yeah. She was a couple of years behind me. I also played football there, which was how her old man knew me. And why he started hiring me to find her when she started disappearing."

"You did a good job this time," snickered Maley.

"She was a girl who liked to kick off her shoes in a hotel room and settle down with a bottle." He shrugged. "*Anybody's* hotel room. I doubt if she even would have drawn a line at an Irishman."

Henry Tekawa cut in quickly, "You're saying she was a lush, not a junkie, Neil? If you'd seen the tracks inside her elbows and on the backs of her knees—"

"No, I'm not saying that. She was a hype, all right. That's the word I picked up down in Mexico City a couple of weeks ago when I followed her trail down there. But it's a recent development—within the past year." He paused, very deliberately. "The word around is that Kolinski's the one who introduced her to the needle. He used to be her old man's chauffeur three, four years ago."

"Convenient," muttered Maley.

"Are you offering this as a possible motive?"

"I'm not offering anything as anything, Hank. I'm giving you what I know. But here's something else I know: Roberta Stayton was a very hard-nosed girl. If she decided to take a cure, and if Kolinski hooked her originally, she could very well have decided to blow the whistle on him. And he could have decided to . . . Christ, Hank, face it: if you hadn't walked in on him, it'd have gone down in the books as an accidental, self-administered O.D. Right?"

"Right. And now all we have to do is figure out who the hell Docker is and where the hell he fits into all this."

"*You* do," corrected Neil Fargo. "Docker's your problem, not mine. Mine is telling old man Stayton he just lost an heir."

"You sound all broken up for him," said Tekawa precisely, like a sparrow eating sunflower seeds.

"He's a tough old bastard, played for the Bears in the thirties. He'll stand up to it. See you at the gym tonight, Hank?"

"Sure." Tekawa went into a karate stance of his own. "I'll set you on your ass."

"Ten bucks says you don't." He paused deliberately. "On that other thing I talked to you about . . ."

"All set to go," said Tekawa smoothly.

When the big detective had departed, the redhead began, "Hank, don't you think maybe we ought to hold—"

Tekawa cut him off with a headshake. "I don't think anything," he said. "Not yet."

Maley nodded judiciously. He said, "You and him

are pretty good friends, I hear. Belong to the same karate studio, trade off phone numbers . . ."

He was very carefully not looking at his partner, but his voice trailed off under Tekawa's grave, unblinking regard. Maley finally met that gaze and his face began to grow pink as if trying to match his hair.

Tekawa said, in a disgusted voice, "Fargo won the Rose Bowl for Stanford his senior year. Played two years with the Forty-Niners and then quit to enlist in the Special Forces. Battlefield promotion to an officer, two tours of duty in Vietnam, resigned from the Army after his enlistment and extension were up. Came back here to go to work as a private investigator with Lipset while going to Hastings Law, nights . . ."

"Look, Henry—"

"Passed the bar after only three years, but never practiced. Set himself up as a p.i. instead, specializing in investigations for attorneys until Maxwell Stayton sort of put him on watchdog duty over the daughter."

"All right, Henry, you've made your point. I just—"

"Fargo's bigger than we are, tougher than we are, he's smarter than at least you are, and he has better connections at City Hall than either of us—as long as Stayton's his client."

"Henry, you don't have to rub it in."

"On top of that, he knows his rights better than we know ours. Now, if you can figure out a way to pry any-thing—anything at all—out of Neil Fargo that he doesn't want to have pried, you let me know. Will you do that, Jerry?"

"Well, sure, I—"

"Otherwise, would you just kindly shut to fuck up?"

The big redheaded cop stared at him hotly. Then both men suddenly began to laugh.

Sixteen

Harsh calipers of pain that had not been there when he had talked with Neil Fargo that morning creased Maxwell Stayton's face. The cold room's glacial light gleamed off his grey hair.

"Yes," he said formally. "That is my daughter. That is Roberta Stayton."

"Thank you, sir," said Inspector Vince Wylie.

The two men turned away. Stayton, though he was at least fifteen years older than the policeman, looked the harder, better-conditioned of the two. Wylie held the door for him. If Stayton heard the rattle of the runners behind them as the attendant slid the body back into its refrigerator drawer, he gave no indication. In the hallway outside the viewing room, he stopped. One way led to the entrance off Ahern Alley where the morgue wagons delivered their goods; the other led back to the Coroner's business office through which they'd come.

"You are a Homicide inspector, is that right?"

"Yes, sir."

"In charge of the investigation of my daughter's murder?"

"Her death. Yes, sir."

Stayton frowned at the change of emphasis Wylie had made, but did not comment on it. Instead, he remarked, "I understood that personnel from the Coroner's office, not from the police department, displayed bodies for identification purposes."

Wylie was suddenly uncomfortable.

"Well, you see, sir, I . . . ah . . ."

"You wanted to see if I'm as cold a son of a bitch as I'm supposed to be. I am, Inspector. You'd do well to remember that."

Wylie was no longer abashed. "I'm conducting an investigation into an alleged murder, Mr. Stayton. You were apprised of your daughter's demise by a civilian instead of authorized police personnel. This—"

"Neil Fargo," agreed Stayton. "And this robbed you of a chance to study my reactions, to judge whether my surprise at news of her death was genuine or not. A daughter who was a—what is the term, a hype?—could be a great embarrassment for a man in my position, and the man who murdered her is an ex-employee. So you decided to retrieve what you could of the situation by studying my reactions to seeing her dead body. Is that so?"

"Something like that, yes, sir."

Stayton nodded. "I've seen dead bodies before. What is happening with Alex Kolinski?"

Wylie moved up the hall, the industrialist falling in beside him. A greedy light had entered the cop's eyes.

"I believe he is going through the booking process, Mr. Stayton. But I can arrange for you to speak privately with him if you—"

"I don't want to see the bastard. I just want to make sure he gets strung up by the nuts."

Without waiting for a reply, Stayton opened the door which led into the narrow room, desk-crowded, which was behind the Coroner's office reception counter. Wylie held back.

"I understand there was friction between you and Kolinski while he was in your employ."

"I found him screwing my daughter while he was my chauffeur, and kicked his ass out of my house. I suppose you could call that friction."

They went through the narrow office, past the civil service stenos typing like aged arthritics, and out to the broad concrete ramp from the Hall of Justice to the Harrison Street municipal parking lot. Beyond the lot and above it, the Skyway moaned and shook with the beginnings of the rush-hour traffic.

"One other little thing has bothered me, sir," said Wylie.

Stayton, who had been starting down the ramp toward the lot, turned resignedly back. The air was chilly, for the sun was low above the soft, maimed breasts of Twin Peaks; but it was not nearly as chilly as the air in the room they had just quit. Stayton, in a suit but without a topcoat, seemed impervious to both sorts of cold.

"What is that?" he asked impatiently.

"This thing of Neil Fargo calling you about your daughter's death."

"He is in my employ. I expect loyalty of my employees."

"If that loyalty should conflict with the police in their authorized investigations—"

"Then the police have legal remedies. Meanwhile, you've been a policeman long enough to know the power realities of this city. I am one of those realities, and my daughter is dead. The man who made her dead will pay the full penalty of the law."

"And if he *didn't* make her dead?" demanded Wylie stubbornly.

"If you have doubts as to Kolinski's guilt, dismiss them. They are puerile. Get in the way of his conviction for murder in the first degree, and I will crush you, utterly."

The planes of Wylie's rather ugly face tightened and flattened. Unconsciously, he set his feet as if to take or deliver a blow. He said thinly, "Are you threatening a police officer, Mr. Stayton?"

"It is not a threat." He laid a finger against the middle button of Wylie's honest, off-the-rack suit. "It is a statement of objective fact. Utterly, if you interfere."

He turned on his heel and strode down the ramp. Below, in a red-curbed zone where no cars were allowed to park, his long black sleek Continental waited, the chauffeur stiff beside the open back door. Wylie watched the grey-haired industrialist get in. The door shut with a sound like a vault being closed. The car pulled away with the noise of autumn leaves being drifted by the wind.

Wylie looked at his outstretched right hand. The outspread fingers were tremoring. He said, "Shit," aloud, and got out a cigarette. As he hunched over it and his match, drawing in the fragrant harsh smoke, a voice spoke lightly behind him.

"And that's today's word from God. Stay tuned for the Bay Area weather."

"You heard that bastard?"

Henry Tekawa nodded. He was lounged against the pipe railing in lofty disdain of soot and dirt. He said, "You have to make allowances, Vince. The man *has* lost a daughter."

"And found a son named Neil Fargo," he sneered. He cursed several times in a tired voice, then shook his head. "You looking for me?"

"I understand you have an A.P.B. out for somebody named Docker."

"Somebody named Docker is right. That's all we got on him, a lot of good the A.P.B.'s going to do. Homicide this morning out on Bryant Street. Just the last name, no initials, no prints, nothing in R&I. Material witness at the moment. Why?"

"I've got a sort of informant named Docker. Just the last name, no initials—"

"Jesus Christ," said Wylie. "I'm buying the coffee."

They rode the elevator to the Hall of Justice basement and the low-roofed, pale-walled public cafeteria across from the personal property room of the city jail. They found a corner table away from the attorneys and their clients, and where they had a chance of not being spotted by any newsmen working the police beat.

"You have a package on the dead man? Marquez?" Tekawa's flat-planed face was politely interested, nothing more.

"He's a Mexican national. We've teletyped, but . . ."

"Could he have been a drug courier?"

"Hey." Wylie was silent, considering. They drank coffee. "That's cute. I'll tell you something, Hank. Addison, the cat we found unconscious at the scene, is a chemist. We don't have a package on him, but . . ."

"Marquez brings it in, Addison tests it for purity," mused Tekawa. "When Docker told me that Kolinski was giving somebody an O.D., he was very specific. It was a hotshot of pure skag hijacked at Bryant Street this morning. Said a courier got killed and that you were handling the case."

"Any question at all that Kolinski *didn't* hit her?"

"I just had the fingerprint report on that syringe. Kolinski, no question." Tekawa's grin was pure pleasure. He parted forefinger and index finger to hold the hypo, with his thumb depressed the imaginary plunger. "Like that. If the autopsy confirms overdose, he did it."

"But then where does that fucking Docker fit in?"

"Where does he fit in down at Bryant Street?"

Wylie told him, all of it.

When he was finished, Henry Tekawa said, "There any suggestion of dope, besides the chemist being there?"

"Well . . . Rosas, the hype they collared there, picked up that speed from the medicine chest. And another ampule of speed was busted on the bathroom floor that he says he didn't drop. So there could of been more, and Docker could have used it. That boy is cutting a wide enough swath to read like somebody on *something.*"

"And prints on the shards of the broken ampule?"

"No."

"Wiped?"

"Rubber gloves. Again, in my book, Docker. I've reconstructed what I think are his movements after he left Bryant Street at seven-thirty this morning. He'd already killed Marquez with his bare hands, and roughed up Addison. Now he roughs up Rosas in Franklin Square, tries to set him up for the fall on the Marquez wipe. Next, two spade baggage-handlers down at Greyhound give his description as the cat who beat hell out of a little hanger-on named Rowlands—only he told the spades he was a syndicate enforcer."

"Are you sure it's the same man?" asked Tekawa.

"Description fits. An hour, hour-and-a-half later a guy with the same description shows up on Market and First, stomps some hippie chick's toes, comes on heavy in a First Street bar, then buys a one-way bus ticket to L.A. on Trailways. Then—"

"Did he get a bus ticket at Greyhound?"

"Yeah. I forgot that. Seattle. One-way."

The voices at the next table rose sharply enough to cut into their discussion. One of the men was hawk-nosed, heavy-jawed, with greying dark hair brushed straight back. He wore oddly-assorted clothing: a yellow knit pull-over t-shirt, black narrow shoes, one black and one brown sock, pyjama bottoms, and a yellow sport shirt that didn't go with anything else, especially the pajamas.

". . . don't *know* when I can pay you back the bail money, Dave!"

"How the hell did you end up in the slam in the first place?" Dave was younger, long-haired, with a mechanic's grease permanently imbedded beneath his fingernails.

"Had a fight with the old lady and she swung at me with a butcher knife so I called the cops. But they came and took *me*. And the landlord was raising hell, I don't know what his beef is, I've been there six years, he gets thirty-one dollars a week from me, he's got a good thing going . . ."

They became aware of the cops' scrutiny, lowered their voices. Wylie shook his head. "There's some fucking compensations to being plainclothes at that, Hank. We don't have to break up domestic beefs. Anyway, a few minutes after Docker bought this bus ticket at Trailways—which he didn't use—a black hanger-on named Browne got the shit beat out of him in the men's can there. We can't tie it strictly to Docker, and Browne ain't talking, just like Rowlands, but . . ."

"But," said Henry Tekawa in a disgruntled voice. "None of it makes much sense, does it? Weird mixture of irrationality and cunning. And none of it ties in with a heroin O.D. in a Tenderloin hotel . . ."

"Wait . . . a . . . minute . . ." exclaimed Wylie with narrowed eyes. "There was a Mexican figurine busted on the floor at Bryant Street. Would of been hollow when it was whole—"

"The lab test the pieces for H dust?" demanded Tekawa quickly.

"No, but they sure as fuck will now."

Tekawa said excitedly, "Walter Hariss imports clay figurines from Mexico." Wylie started to interrupt, but he went right on. "Hariss and Alex Kolinski are owners-of-record, according to information I received just this afternoon, of the FarJon Hotel where Roberta Stayton died. And Vice confirms that Kolinski probably has been running a string of junkie whores out of that hotel."

"Roberta Stayton a junkie whore?"

"Little hard to figure, isn't it?" agreed Tekawa. "But according to the black chick who managed the place, she was one of the string—specialized in giving head. She was down to around ninety pounds and her mouth was about the last thing she had left that anybody'd pay to use." Somehow, Tekawa's brutal words were delivered with such utter disinterest that they were robbed of salaciousness or even of offense. They were merely a recital of facts.

"Docker the bagman?" ventured Wylie. "Knocking over his own drop? But even if we fall on him, I doubt like hell if the D.A. can tag him for Murder One on Marquez. No witnesses, he could damn well cop a self-defense plea. Marquez had a gun, fired one shot from it. If Docker had a gun, he didn't use it."

"Apparently didn't need it." Tekawa drained the last of his coffee, made a face at the dissolved sugar in the bottom of the cup. "We don't even know Docker was a bagman, except he carried an attaché case. If someone was making a dope buy at Bryant Street, we don't know who was buying and who was selling. Christ, none of it makes sense."

"There's one other common denominator," said Wylie almost slyly.

"I was wondering when you'd get around to him."

"Yeah. Neil Fargo. He rents the Bryant Street flat a couple of weeks ago to stash a witness—he says—and shows up at the Jones Street hotel where the Stayton woman gets it." He looked suddenly disgruntled. "Trouble is, he was screwing some Swedish chick this morning when the action was taking place at Bryant Street. And you were already there when he got to Jones Street."

"And he had a legitimate reason to be there," said Tekawa. "According to Stayton's personal secretary—who doesn't like Fargo any more than you do—he's been hired three times in the past two-and-a-half years to find Roberta Stayton after she's wandered off with somebody she picked up in a bar or at a ski lodge or whatever."

"How long was he looking for her this time?"

"Three weeks, part of it in Mexico, according to what he says."

"Kinda sloppy work for a private eye with his reputation, ain't it? With her marching up and down Jones Street under a sandwich board labelled 'Come and Get It'?"

"You said yourself you wouldn't figure Maxwell Stayton's daughter to be a junkie whore."

"There's that." Wylie's face was sullen. "Hell, if we could just uncover something to prove that Fargo and Docker know each other—"

"If if if!" Henry Tekawa threw up his hands in abrupt atypical frustration. "All we have is if's. What we need is to lay our hands on Docker."

Seventeen

"What we need is to lay our hands on Docker, and damned fast!" Walter Hariss pointed a soft-tipped finger at Neil Fargo for emphasis. The inner office of the Bush Street parking garage smelled of too many cigars smoked in too confined a space.

Neil Fargo leaned against the frame of the door he

had just opened, and laughed in the importer's face. He had his hands thrust into the pockets of his overcoat.

"I fail to see what's so funny."

"You are. We are. We're running around in tight little circles, Docker's laying back laughing at us all. Kolinski's in the slammer."

"In jail? For what? I don't understand."

Neil Fargo straightened away from the door frame, the sardonic grin still on his face. "The big it. Murder One."

"Mur . . . But that's insane! He just left here an hour ago—"

"For the FarJon Hotel. Murder One, Walt." His eyes gleamed with delight. "The cops walked in on him just as he was feeding a massive overdose to a junkie whore named Robin."

Walter Hariss was on his feet. His face was chalky, then, as he spoke, became mottled with congested blood.

"Overdose to . . . to Robin? She's . . ."

"That's right, Walt. Roberta Stayton is dead." Spurious concern came into his eyes. "What's the matter? Your humanitarian feeling for her—"

"But . . . but . . . Alex wouldn't . . . He knew what I planned to . . ."

He stopped speaking abruptly. Neil Fargo's voice was very soft. "What did you plan for her, Walt, that you forgot to tell me about? Like you forgot to tell me where she was?"

But fear had entered the importer's face and voice which far outweighted any fear he may have felt of Neil Fargo. "It must have been Docker!"

"The fuzz think it was Kolinski."

"No, I tell you, it was Docker!" Sweat was starting out on his face. "He . . . must have framed Alex for it. Must have known—"

"The police have Kolinski cold, Walt. The spade chick on the desk is nailing his nuts to the wall every time she opens her mouth."

"She . . ." Hariss licked his lips. "Has she mentioned . . . ah . . ."

"The fact that you're half owner of that hotel?" Neil

Fargo shook his head. "I wouldn't know. But I did."

"You—"

"Sure. I checked with the tax assessor's office this afternoon." His voice and eyes hardened. "You had to be cute, not let me know you had Roberta Stayton under your control. You think I was going to stand still for that?" He laughed harshly. "You'll come out okay, Kolinski's the one who was running the girls out of there. You can just throw him to the wolves, since they have him on Murder One already, and end up with the whole pie."

Hariss had gotten control of himself once more. He sat down heavily in the chair behind the desk. His features were once more impassive.

"I'll do what has to be done. But if that nigger says Alex gave an overdose to Robin Stayton, she's lying and it's a frame. Docker himself was at that hotel less than two hours ago!"

"Docker . . ." Neil Fargo's eyes were slits. "Are you *sure?* He . . ." Suddenly his face cleared. "Yeah," he muttered to himself. He said: "Who gave you that hot rocket?"

Hariss started to speak, then stopped. He was suddenly troubled. "The nigger."

"She called you up? Told Kolinski that Docker was there?"

Hariss nodded reluctantly, as if only then beginning to see what the other man apparently already had seen.

"You listened in on the other phone?"

This time Hariss shook his head. His face had gotten gloomy. Neil Fargo clapped his hands together once, palm on palm, like a child playing pattycake. He left the open doorway for the first time, sat down across the desk from Hariss.

"So you don't know Docker was there, you only know the black chick *said* he was there. And you don't even know the black chick said he was there, you only know Kolinski *told* you that's what she said."

"Why would he lie? When Alex left here he wasn't planning to kill anyone. He wanted information that Roberta Stayton had."

"Which was?"

"Docker's current whereabouts."

"For all you know," said Neil Fargo patiently, "it was Roberta Stayton herself on the phone. And she may have threatened Kolinski with something—anything. Some sort of exposure. He knew he had to take her out, fast, so he left here with a hotshot in his pocket—"

"We didn't have any pure stuff," Hariss objected. His eyes blazed with sudden, almost feminine anger. "Your friend Docker saw to that."

"Walt, get it through your head: Kolinski killed her, for whatever reason. There just isn't any doubt about it. As for the rest of it, Docker probably *was* there. The spade chick says he was. And it was Docker who tipped the cops about Kolinski and the overdose."

"There you are." Hariss seemed only to have heard the part of it which fit his preconceptions. "Docker is playing some devious game of his own, aimed at crucifying me."

"So far you haven't come out too bad," said Neil Fargo. "It's Kolinski who's in the soup."

"Indeed? My courier dead, my chemist compromised —and my Mexican sources are not going to be in any hurry to start dealing with me again. And it was Alex who had the street distribution net arranged, not me."

"So get the street layout from him on visiting day," said Neil Fargo callously. "This idea that Docker is out to get you just doesn't make sense. He doesn't even know you, doesn't even know your *name*—at least not from me."

"From Roberta Stayton, then. He must have known her, if he was able to direct the police to her room."

"Yeah, probably. But he didn't mention Roberta by name when he tipped the cops—just Kolinski. Kolinski was O.D.'ing *somebody*. And what reason would he have to be going after you, for Chrissake? He already got the heroin and the money that was going to buy it. He's already fucked you and fucked me." His voice became momentarily strident, as if infected with Hariss' tension. "What's he hanging around for?" He sneered suddenly. "He doesn't like your face? Shit, I don't like it either, Hariss, but I can live with it . . ."

The ringing phone cut him off.

"Bush Street Garage," said Hariss.

An old cracked voice asked suspiciously, "Is Neil Fargo there?"

"One moment, I'll check. I'm just the car-park boy." Hariss held his hand over the receiver, pointed toward the wall phone over the safe.

Neil Fargo lifted the receiver, said, "Yeah, speaking."

"You put out the word on a yellow Mercury Montego, license six-three-six, Zee-Eff-Eff?"

"One moment," snapped Hariss. He punched the HOLD button so the caller could not pick up any of their conversation. He exclaimed, in red-hot fury, "You bastard, you had that license number and—"

"It came in after Rizzato dropped around to my office," said Neil Fargo. He stared hard at Hariss. After a moment, Hariss' gaze faltered. He punched back into the outside line. Neil Fargo said into the phone, "That's right. You have anything on it?"

"It just gassed up a few minutes ago at the Standard station on Tenth Street."

"Which station? Tenth and Folsom?"

"That's the one. Left the station heading south for the freeway on-ramp—"

"You get a look at the driver?"

"Big blond fellow with glasses. Hornrims, like. Long hair like he was one of them TV stars or something. 'Cept'n he had a limp he sorta tried to hide . . ."

"Did he have an attaché case with him?" demanded Hariss.

If the oldster noticed this was not Neil Fargo's voice, he apparently didn't care.

"Was one down behind the front seat, like. I noticed it when he got in the car. Y'know, he hadda open the door and—"

Neil Fargo cut in, "We don't need your life history, old man. He say anything about where he was headed?"

"Asked which off-ramp he took to San Francisco International Airport."

"Come by the office tomorrow, your envelop'll be there," said Neil Fargo, and hung up.

"The airport!" exclaimed Hariss. "He's finally trying to skip." There was a tinge of relief in his voice. "We can . . ."

He ran down because Neil Fargo had jerked the snubbynose .38 policeman's special from its belt holster, had flipped out the cylinder with a practiced jerk of his wrist so he could check the chambers. All were full; the detective apparently did not carry one empty under the hammer for safety. He looked up, caught the importer's eye.

"You can reach Kolinski's people covering the airport?"

"Yes, but—"

"How many are there?"

He thought a moment. "Four."

"Good. All right, one in a stalled car on the airport turnoff overpass, so he can check that Docker actually enters the airport grounds. And a yellow Montego won't be hard to spot from up there if Docker was bullshitting and just keeps going south. One man at the head of the escalators in both the North and South terminals. They can also watch the street entry doors in case he just dumps the car in a loading zone and leaves it there. That leaves a man free to coordinate between terminals."

Hariss considered for a moment. "Yes, I see that. But—"

Neil Fargo had snapped the gun shut. "But, shit! Nobody tries to take him." He shoved the gun back into its holster. His voice was filled with contempt. "Your fucking people have gone up against him three times today, if we count Bryant Street, and he's wiped their asses for them each time. Just have them keep tabs on him until I get there."

"And what if he happens to get on an airplane before you get there?" demanded Hariss acidly.

"He won't. It's the middle of the rush hour, he's on an unfamiliar freeway—he won't be making much time. Besides, he's not getting on any airplane with that attaché case. He wouldn't be able to get it by the anti-hijack security guards."

The detective departed without waiting for an answer, but then swerved across the garage to Hariss' waiting Fleetwood. The driver's window was down, and Neil Fargo leaned on the frame.

He said to Rizzato, "You're a dead man tomorrow morning if you're still in San Francisco. Remember that."

Rizzato said nothing, but spat deliberately against the side of the Fairlane as it went by him and out into the traffic-jammed lanes of Bush Street. In the office, Walt Hariss had relayed Neil Fargo's plan to his airport contact; but there had been significant changes in the instructions. He sat for a full minute behind the desk, eyes hooded, as if reviewing his battle plan.

Then he arose abruptly, went to the door to signal Rizzato. He was rotating a fresh cigar in his lighter flame when the chauffeur appeared in the doorway. Hariss outlined it all for him: the arrest of Kolinski, the telephone call from Neil Fargo's informant, the detective's instructions for the men at the airport and his abrupt departure there.

"I want you to get down there as quick as you can, Gus. On the white courtesy telephone page a man named Nolan Avery. He will tell you whether Docker has arrived, where he is, what he's doing."

Gus Rizzato showed his yellowish teeth in a grin. "Instead of telling Fargo. Beautiful!"

"Most important, Avery will tell you where Docker parked. Wait for him at his car, take the attaché case away from him. You ought to be able to manage it, he's never laid eyes on you. He'll park in the garage directly across from the terminal, I'm sure."

"But if he gets on a plane, Mr. Hariss . . ."

"Docker isn't going to check that attaché case, and he will also be unable to carry it aboard any plane without having it opened and searched by the security guards. Once he realizes that, he will have to return to his car."

"And that's when I get the attaché case." Rizzato's eyes had brightened at the prospect.

"Be careful of him, Gus. From everything we've heard, he's fast and ruthless."

"He's a gimp, right. Mr. Hariss?"

"A fast gimp, Gus. Believe me, he—"

Rizzato repeated the single blazingly fast movement behind his neck to have the commando knife lying in his hand, as he had done in front of Pamela Gardner earlier that day. His lips pursed in silent laughter.

"He'll never see it coming, Mr. Hariss."

Walter Hariss nodded. "Into my hands, Gus, that attaché case. My hands only."

Rizzato reversed his lightning movement, and the knife was back in its neck sheath. He paused in the doorway.

"What about Neil Fargo, Mr. Hariss?"

"Yes, he's a problem, isn't he? Apparently he's fond of that secretary of his." He thought for a moment; then his eyes cleared. He chuckled. "We're forgetting. Fargo must account for a large sum of money he will be unable to account for—to someone whom he fears. That means someone who is tougher than Fargo himself. By tomorrow morning his major concern will be staying alive, not avenging what you did in his office."

Rizzato grinned. He rolled his shoulders to make the padded suitcoat sit better on his narrow sinewy frame. "Fair enough, Mr. Hariss."

After he was gone, Walter Hariss went to the door, peered out. He waited until he saw the overweight Rock Hudson named Blaney, and crooked a finger at him. Blaney, whose regular job was running the night crew, appeared in the doorway wearing a white knee-length smock. Outside, the three car-parkers were bringing down a steady stream of commuter cars for their homeward-bound owners.

"I have some bad news, Blaney." He gestured the big man into a chair across the desk. "Cigar?"

"Don't mind if I do, Mr. Hariss."

"Alex Kolinski is in jail. He was arrested this afternoon in the act of giving an overdose of heroin to a girl in a Tenderloin hotel."

Blaney was shocked. He dropped the cigar, had to root around on the unswept floor to find it again. He came erect. "Alex? Busted?"

"They have him cold, according to my information. Now, I know you have always worked for Alex, and I'm sure you hold him in the same sort of esteem that I do. On the other hand, business must continue." He paused as if inviting comment from the big man across the desk. None was forthcoming. Hariss nodded. "I'm sure that you were sufficiently in Alex's confidence to know that I have a discreet financial interest in this garage."

"Sure. Half-owner."

"There you are," said Hariss delightedly. "I want to assure you, Blaney, that the situation here at the garage will remain stable while Alex is . . . away."

"I'm glad to hear that, Mr. Hariss."

Hariss leaned forward, bringing his heavy ruddy features into the circle of light cast by the desk lamp. "I would like to feel that in the eventuality of Alex's permanent . . . absence, I could count on your primary loyalties lying with the . . . um, partnership instead of with Alex himself. Who, after all created the trouble in which he now finds himself."

Blaney leaned forward himself. His lips curved under the heavy mustache. "You're here, Mr. Hariss. Alex ain't."

"Admirably put. One other point, Blaney. Alex had certain . . . outside activities having to do with the projected distribution of a certain highly-lucrative commodity. I'm sure Alex had a . . . buffer, someone to stand between himself and the street people—who can be unstable and need stern handling from time to time."

"Yeah," said Blaney. He sat utterly still, flat-faced, considering. He smiled again. "Yeah. I know who they are, and I'm the man who deals with them."

"I feel that shortly I will have a kilo of ninety-five percent pure which should be cut and . . . offered for sale."

Blaney began, "I thought that was . . ." Then caught himself and stopped.

"Alex's arrest has changed that situation," said Hariss smoothly. "Our best interests now will be served by distributing this commodity ourselves rather than selling it as a unit elsewhere as an expedient toward raising more cash."

Blaney's voice tightened hopefully. "I'll need a percentage."

"Were you to get a percentage from Alex?"

After an appreciable pause, the big man shook his head. "Lump sum."

"You'll get a percentage from me."

"Hey!" he exclaimed, as if he had run a bluff and had won. "That's swell, Mr. Hariss."

When Blaney had returned to the garage floor, Harris laughed to himself. "A percentage—and of course standing between me and danger if anything goes wrong." He laughed again, softly. "And of course *no* percentage of the money in the attaché case that the money man will be taking out of Neil Fargo's hide."

He dialled his home number, told his daughter to come and pick him up. Then he leaned back in his chair with the contemplative face of a man with a clear conscience and good digestion who has supper on his mind. His wife had recently hired an excellent cook.

Eighteen

Some twenty minutes before Walter Hariss had telephoned his daughter, Docker had driven the yellow Montego up onto the San Francisco Skyway. Not at Tenth and Folsom as the tipster had informed Neil Fargo and Hariss, however; he had entered the concrete maze at Gough and Turk Streets. Freeway is a misnomer during rush-hour traffic; almost instantly, Docker was in the stop-and-go tie-up where the Oak Street on-ramp poured fresh commuters into the Central Freeway's main stream.

Docker edged the powerful car into the right lane after the South Van Ness/Tenth Street influx had been assimilated, then spent five motionless minutes before he could begin edging forward again.

The delay did not seem to unduly frustrate the hulking blond man, although he did keep a nervous tattoo of muscular fingers going on the steering wheel. His inner tension displayed itself in other ways, too. His bleak eyes behind their hornrims kept searching the cars massed in the growing twilight behind him, and every minute or two he would jam the radio station-selector in search of relief from the mindless rush-hour commercials.

Finally the yellow Montego was past the tight-jammed lanes which went east toward Bay Bridge, and he was able to take the one-lane concrete loop which put him into the main traffic stream south. After he'd left the monstrous concrete spaghetti of the Southern Freeway interchange behind, he was able to touch the posted 50 m.p.h. for the first time as holes began appearing among the solid lanes of cars on the Bayshore; Interstate 280 had siphoned off the westbound traffic.

Docker reached 65 m.p.h. and began paying even more attention to the rear-view mirror after the South San Francisco off-ramp, but then abruptly abandoned the surveillance.

"Couldn't spot a tail in this traffic anyway," he muttered aloud.

He lit a cigarette, which kept his face busy and perhaps his mind as well. His harsh features were illuminated from below by the dashboard lights. His calloused, deadly hands were rock-solid on the wheel except when he moved the dwindling cigarette around in his mouth.

After the San Bruno off-ramp ten miles south of the city, he got into the right-hand lane reserved for the airport turn-off a mile-and-a-half further on. The big yellow car, slowed to a decorous thirty, went by a stalled motorist on the overpass who had his hood raised and a plastic Highway Patrol *already helped* pennant impaled on his radio aerial.

Ahead of Docker were the ever-changing auto traffic

patterns heading toward the twin terminals, each lane now marked with its special destination. Behind, his rear-view mirror showed him, the stalled motorist was slamming down his hood, sprinting around his car for the driver's side.

Docker smiled grimly to himself. His big hands swerved the auto into the left-hand, PARKING lanes. His foot suddenly goosed the accelerator and the car went into a three-quarters slide right under the INCOMING PLANES ramp and down a narrow blacktop lane which led to the lowest tier of the parking garage.

This won him precious seconds. No lights showed in his rear-view mirror as he collected from the automatic ticket machine, drove under the electronically-folding restraint arm, fast, then stood the car on its nose a dozen yards beyond.

Across half a lane coming in from the right were sawhorses, which bore the sign: LEVEL FULL. USE RAMP TO UPPER FLOORS.

Docker twisted the power-assisted wheel over hard, shot past the sawhorses, almost instantly made a hard left into the intersecting lane. He drove forward three car lengths, stopped, killing lights and motor in the same moment.

The Montego was now in a lane parallel to the entry land and hidden from any car coming through the ticket machines.

Docker left the car, crept unevenly forward between parked cars, squatted down so his head would not show above them. A bare ten seconds later a car nosed down the ramp, collected a ticket. Docker grinned tightly. It was the stalled motorist's green Plymouth.

The Plymouth hesitated at the sawhorses. Docker was tense. The Plymouth finally went on. Docker relaxed. He came partially erect so he could watch over the hood of one of the parked cars as it went up the ramp.

It didn't. It went past, on toward the next intersecting lane down the garage which was parallel to that which was sawhorsed.

Docker ran unevenly back to the Montego, kicked it

alive, squealed back to the sawhorse lane, swung quickly back into the main aisle down which the Plymouth had just gone.

Ahead, the Plymouth had already disappeared down one of the cross-lanes.

Docker followed. For the next three minutes he criss-crossed the entire floor, always a lane behind the Plymouth as it made its slow search, able to follow its progress by watching for the oblong of plastic forgotten on the aerial over the roofs of the intervening rows of parked cars.

Finally the Plymouth tired of the search and went up the ramp out of sight. Docker parked in an open space under a NO PARKING sign and directly below the immense air blower which served to ventilate the garage.

He retrieved his attaché case from behind the seat, carefully locked the car. He was at the very end of the dimly-lit garage, half a city block from the closest moving sidewalk which carried passengers to the sub-floor of the Central, older of the two terminals.

Docker limped right by this oasis of escalators, stairs and elevator to the upper garage floors, ignoring the glaring fluorescents and canned mechanical voice tolling the airlines which could be reached by this conveyor belt.

Instead, he went most of the length of the garage to the second, similar complex which carried people by escalator belt from the upper floors and by conveyor belt from this floor, under the two-tiered street outside, to the Southern Terminal.

Docker waited inconspicuously between parked cars until the down-ramps disgorged a group of five servicemen, two of them in civvies. Docker didn't really blend in with them because of the length of his hair, but he did get protective coloration from them.

At the far end of the moving sidewalk were escalator stairs up to the luggage and transportation level, then yet another escalator to the terminal main floor.

He seemed to be with a woman and a three-year-old baby getting off the escalator in the immense expanse of waiting area, by staying a tight three paces behind them as they angled over toward the newsstand in the center of the building.

Despite this a youth with a bad complexion, and the sort of scraggly beard so often worn to mask a receding chin, glanced up sharply from his comic book when Docker passed. The youth was sitting on one of the black Naugahyde chairs that flanked the escalator.

He sighed, folded his comic book, stuck it in the back pocket of his jeans as he stood up. By chance he wandered in the direction of the newsstand.

Beyond the newsstand, and enclosed on three sides by glass walls to discourage rip-offs, were several rows of paperback book shelves. Docker threaded his way through browsers and time-killers to the rear of the bookracks, where he stood with his back to the glass wall and scanned the crowds for a full two minutes.

Apparently he saw nothing to disturb him. He bought a candy bar, went down to the central cluster of departure gates munching it, then entered a small dark intimate bar under the huge departure board.

Here he found a table facing the door, ordered and sipped a tall pilsener glass of draft beer while agreeing with the comments of the short-skirted waitress about the freeway accident by South San Francisco which apparently had tied up all the south-bound lanes. He left too much silver on the table, lounged under the departure sign for two more minutes, then limped down the corridor to the nearest men's room. Another three minutes there.

After all this, Docker went back through the main terminal and outside to the ARRIVALS curb, where he stood weighing up the various uniformed porters. He finally selected one, talked with him. A twenty-dollar bill changed hands.

Docker went back inside, this time to cross directly to American Airlines and queue up at the PURCHASE TICKETS HERE window. Waiting, he set the attaché case between his feet, toed it along ahead of him as the line inched forward.

Eventually the overweight blonde in stretch pants and

mink coat stepped aside with her ticket. Docker returned the smile of the well-groomed, uniformed, utterly forgettable young man behind the chest-high counter, and accepted his offer of aid.

"I'd like," he said precisely as he looked down to toe his attaché case forward again, "a ticket to—*hey!*"

On the final word he turned quickly, stepping back so his heel came down firmly on the foot of the youth with the scraggly beard and comic book. Somehow the attaché case slid six feet across the floor in the process. Because Docker was whirling with such energy at the same time that the youth was anchored firmly in his path, his elbow struck the captive a numbing blow in the chest.

"*My attaché case!*" Docker was yelling and pointing. "*He tried to steal my attaché case!*"

The boy was staggering back, mouth open to yell protests. Docker stumbled as he did, apparently losing his balance because of his suddenly very noticeable bad leg. To save himself, he reached out to grab the youth's jacket front with both hands.

Somehow, in passing, the hands clapped the boy smartly and simultaneously on each side of the head. Not hard enough to rupture the ear drums but hard enough to compress them sharply.

The boy did what any normal person would do in such a situation. He screamed.

His scream so disconcerted Docker that the big man lost his footing, sprawled full length on the floor. His outstretched hand closed firmly around the handle of the attaché case. People were exclaiming, jostling. Uniformed security guards were converging.

"All right, what happened—"

"What's going . . ."

Docker, struggling to rise, had a grip on the boy's belt. The boy was still yelling. Docker was shouting about his attaché case. The guard trying to help him up was pointing out that the attaché case was in Docker's other hand. The other guard had hold of the boy by this time.

"That kid tried to *grab* my case," Docker finally got out.

"I didn't!" The boy had stopped yelling, was rubbing his ears. "I was just standin' there . . ."

". . . knocked me down, ask these people . . ."

". . . pushed that man, I saw . . ."

". . . bad leg . . ."

"Quiet!" roared one guard. He got a semblance of it. "Now, who saw what happened? *Really* saw, not just heard the commotion?"

A bland-faced black porter pushed forward through the crowd.

"I saw it, officer." He spoke almost apologetically. "It's like the gen'man says. He was in line, went to move his case with his foot, an' this here kid's hand was jes' pullin' it away. He try to grab it, the kid shove 'im . . ."

The guard turned to the hippie youth firmly in the grasp of the other guard. The boy's mouth was still spilling protests and his eyes had become almost frantic with the realization of what was happening.

"That's it, son," said the guard.

"He hired that porter . . ."

"Oh, Christ!" said the guard in a disgusted voice. Docker, meanwhile, had been tapping his watch, shaking his head, backing away. He said, "I'm going to miss my plane if I remain here any longer."

The guard seemed to not realize he had bought no ticket. "Hey, but wait a minnit, mister. You—"

"I'm sure this gentleman can furnish the full particulars."

"Mos' surely can," supplied the porter.

"But . . ."

"I'll be back from Los Angeles tomorrow, officer, then I will be fully prepared to prefer charges against this young beast."

"Well, but . . ."

"Officer, my plane . . ."

The hippie youth's eyes were murderous, but there was no way he could follow. Docker, still casting worried looks at his watch, had pulled an empty plane ticket folder from an inner pocket and was consulting it assiduously as he moved off. His gestures and movements were precisely gauged to mime harassed worry without tipping over into parody.

At the far end of the terminal from American Airlines was a long ramp which slanted down one floor to the baggage area. It was directly beside one of the corridors to the waiting planes, so Docker, now well out of sight of guards, hippie and porter, skipped down the ramp.

The only person who reacted in any way was a short, worried, pudgy man in an almost electric green suit. He chanced to unglue himself from the wall as Docker passed, entered the phone booth he had been standing beside, dropped his dime and began dialling.

Docker went through the gate and past the revolving baggage carrousels, past the deplaned passengers clucking over their luggage like hens around scattered feed, and down the escalator to the moving sidewalk. Two minutes later he was back on the ground floor of the parking garage.

He did not head off toward the yellow Montego directly, however. Instead, he went around to the far side of the huge concrete shaft housing the escalators, stairway, and slow groaning elevator to the upper floors. He punched the elevator button.

As he did, the short, out-of-breath man in the electric green suit came pounding around the corner of the housing, saw him, and pulled up short.

"Ah . . . going up?" he asked Docker with a lame bright smile.

"Level C," said Docker.

They got on the elevator together. The automatic doors slid shut. As they did, Docker's big hands closed around the little man's throat. Skillful fingers found the carotid artery, and the little man went to sleep between Level A and Level B. Docker deposited him on Level C, left him slumbering in an artfully arranged cardiac arrest position, returned to the ground floor, and limped his way down the great empty echoing garage to his Montego.

It was dark in the corner where he had parked it. He stood well clear of the car, in shadow himself, for nearly a minute, head up, eyes questing. It could almost be imagined that his nostrils quivered for the smell of danger.

Finally he shrugged, an almost sheepish expression on his face, and went over to the car. As he bent to unlock the door, shoes scraped concrete behind him. He whirled.

Walking toward him was a small, dark man who could not have been over five-two. His black hair gleamed in the dim light and was slicked straight back. He wore a suit with very wide lapels and a necktie which was even wider.

"Is that your car, sir?" he asked.

"Uh . . . rental," said Docker. He had the car key in his right hand, the attaché case in his left, and no hands left over to do anything about the small, dark man who seemed to be some sort of official.

"Didn't you see the No Parking sign, sir?"

"Well, uh, officer, to tell the truth . . ."

"Parking Authority. Security Division," said the man importantly. His eyes glittered. He stepped closer. "I'll have to see your identification, sir . . ."

He was a yard away. He'd started to extend his hand, stopped abruptly and jerked it back, at the same time looking up at the ceiling.

"What the devil?" he exclaimed.

He put his hand up to the back of his neck as if to feel the water or whatever it was that apparently had dripped on him from the lower concrete above their heads. Docker's face obediently turned upward, apparently in the almost automatic reaction the small man's actions called for.

As it did, Rizzato's hand darted downward in a blur of motion, gripping the commando knife he had just jerked from its neck sheath.

Nineteen

When Gus Rizzato had arrived at San Francisco International, he had first sought out a white courtesy telephone as instructed, had duly spoken to Nolan Avery —who was a short, rotund, worried-looking man in a green suit.

"He's here now," Nolan Avery had said. "He's having a beer in that little bar off the South Terminal concourse."

"Where's his car?"

"Bottom level, down at the north end under the air blower in a No Parking area. Our man missed it first time around, but went back—"

"All right, I'll page you again in a few minutes, give you a phone number. You call me there when Docker starts back for his car. Got that?"

"Yes, sir, Mr. Rizzato." Avery's voice had paused. "That other man, that private detective or whoever he is, hasn't shown up yet."

"Probably still on the freeway. There was a hell of a pileup at South City. I went around, but cars that had gone by that exit before they started the rerouting are stuck until they clear it. He was a few minutes ahead of me, so he's still sitting there." Rizzato had chuckled, then his voice had hardened. "Remember, when he shows up, you tell him nothing. Docker hasn't shown, you've never heard of me. Got that?"

"Yes, Mr. Rizzato."

Now Gus Rizzato sat in the phone booth, waiting for Docker's return to the parking garage. Nolan Avery had the number. Rizzato's face was composed, without impatience or expectation. He found a pimple under his chin, seemed to take sensual pleasure in popping it and wiping his thumbnail on his trouser leg. Twice, after making sure no one was in sight, he stepped from the booth to draw his knife from his neck sheath with that blinding, practiced speed. When the knife was in his hand, his eyes got a moist, hot look.

The phone rang. Avery's voice said, "Docker's just going down the ramp to the luggage area. I think he's on his way to the garage."

"All right, peel off," snapped Rizzato.

"I'd better follow him to make sure—"

"Peel off."

It took Docker a few minutes longer than it should have, but finally, standing in the shadows a few cars away from the yellow Montego, Rizzato could hear the echoing, uneven footsteps approaching. Docker stopped in the shadows a dozen feet from his car.

Rizzato drew his lips back from his teeth in a mirthless grin, began walking toward the big blond man whom he had never seen before but recognized instantly from the descriptions. He called, "Is that your car, sir?"

Then, in seconds, he was in position. He looked upward to draw Docker's eyes, got his hand on his knife with a casual gesture. Then his arm swept down, the knife now an extension of himself, and drove the blade up under Docker's sternum.

That's when things went wrong.

Docker leaned back, mouth open, to see where whatever had apparently fallen on the small man's head had come from. It should have left his solar plexus beautifully open to attack. But Docker kept right on arching back, past the vertical. As he did, his right foot moved back about eighteen inches and planted itself at right angles to Rizzato. His right knee flexed slightly, taking his weight.

But Rizzato was already driving his knife in and up at the place where Docker's middle had been, face contorted with effort and with a delighted rage. There was no way he could check the lunge, even though Docker's body had moved back just beyond the furthest reach of the knife jab. Rizzato grunted with effort as his blade found only empty air. Docker's left knee already had pumped up to his waist and was snapping his leg straight out.

Docker's big shoe, turned so the side of his foot was parallel to the concrete floor, crashed into Gus Rizzato's chest. The force of the kick smashed the little man against the next car with his arms flailing for balance. The knife went flying, landed a dozen paces away where an overhead fluorescent glared down on it.

Docker got one quick stride toward it, cried out, and crumpled with both hands clutching his apparently traitorous right knee. Rizzato, seeing this, found strength to drag in air, enough to get to the knife and pick it up. He leaned back, gasping, against the side of a car with the knife gleaming dully in his right hand.

"Old . . . war wound, Docker?" he panted mockingly.

Docker was on one knee. The light glinted off his glasses. His head was up, his mouth open, as his left hand scrabbled around for the dropped car keys. His right hand found the handle of the car door to drag him up. He stood with his back to the car, slightly crouched, panting.

"If my knee . . . wasn't fucked up . . ."

"It is, Docker." Rizzato had begun his gradual deadly circling as he moved in for the kill. He was doing what he lived for. He hissed, "It's the fear that does it, Docker, knowing it's coming. The piss'll be running down your leg before I put it into you."

"Can't we . . . deal? The briefcase . . . for . . . for my . . ."

"For your life? I've already got that, Docker." Rizzato made a quick thrusting feint, playing with his man, then leapt back laughing from Docker's clumsy attempt to parry. "Once or twice in the belly, Docker, to soften you up. Then the eyes. Then . . ."

Peeler Rizzato went in low, crouched and terrible and deadly, an exceptional knife-fighter carrying darkness with him like a man come to steal corpses. His face was murderous with delight. He was poised on the balls of his feet, balanced for move and feint and thrust as a boxer is, his vital areas well protected by the outthrust, always weaving blade. He moved it in short, swift slashes, ready now to disable Docker's protective arms.

But that too was a feint. He jabbed instead, suddenly deadly, for the stomach. Somehow Docker, with a quick left-hand sweep and going up on his toes like a matador, was lucky enough to turn arm and blade clumsily aside. The steel rang against the car door.

Frustrated, Peeler sprang back. He weaved, crouched, feinted.

Light gleamed on Docker's long blond hair. He was in a crouch himself now. Rizzato lunged. But somehow Docker was not there, was circling his opponent with his jerky, lopsided step. Able to put full weight on the right knee which, though it still made him limp, seemed to have miraculously recovered its full strength.

Rizzato gave a pattering uneasy step or two.

And Docker laughed. "It's the fear," he said mockingly.

Their circling had carried them away from the cars, out into the open. The garage was deserted. Sudden, almost blind fury flooded across Peeler Rizzato's face. He came bolt upright for a moment, his eyes wild. He sputtered, "You . . . it's . . . you *fucker!*"

On the last word, he lunged.

As he did, Docker gave a tremendous screeching bellow that checked the knifeman's flow of movement for a millisecond of time. In that briefest of instants, Docker's left hand snapped forward so steel fingers could slam shut around Peeler's wrist like a jail sentence. The hand went in and up and around, carrying Peeler's arm with it; Docker's shoulder jolted up under Peeler's elbow but Docker's left hand kept right on going down.

Peeler's elbow was dislocated with a sound like a housewife ripping a dustcloth. The knife rattled on the concrete. The imprisoning hand kept moving, so Peeler perforce followed it screeching with pain.

This brought his face forward and down, into the path of the calloused, awful edge of Docker's other hand, being driven out and up in a backhand lash.

Peeler saw it coming; he died squealing his terror. The knife edge of the hand entered his face just under the nose. Front teeth, violently separated roots and all from the gums, flew out from the little killer's face like popping corn; needles of splintered nasal bone were rammed up into the jelly-like substance of his brain's frontal lobes.

Docker sprang nimbly back, let the dying husk go down face forward. Blood poured across the concrete, spattering the tips of Docker's well-polished shoes. Docker turned and limped blindly away, stood with his bare palm resting on the polished fender of somebody's car. His color was that of a spent distance runner just before he collapses of mild shock and vomits on the cinders.

"He had to die," Docker said aloud.

No one answered him. From behind him came the echoing mechanized voice intoning PLEASE WALK ON AND OFF RAMP.

"HE HAD TO DIE!" Docker shouted at the voice.

The voice continued its mindless litany of instruction. Docker seemed to be coming out of it a little. He took off his glasses, rubbed his eyes. He bent, peered at himself in the car's side mirror. It gave him back a pair of staring, terrified eyes in a dread-filled face.

"Too much blood," he said to the face. "Too many dead." Then he found a hollow laugh. "The little wop took it out of you, didn't he, Docker?"

His image mouthed his own words but did not respond. He nodded solemnly, put back on his glasses, shot a quick look around the garage. Far down the aisle he could see three people walking.

Docker toed the insignificant corpse under the nearest car, wiping his shoe-tips on it in the process, recovered attaché case and car keys. Somewhere a car motor started, throbbed. He saw a car beginning to back out, down by the escalator shaft.

He slipped on his gloves as he got into the Montego, then slid down so the top of his head did not show above the window line. He waited. His precautions were unnecessary. The car turned up one of the aisles leading to the exit ramp before getting down to his end of the garage.

Before leaving, Docker got back out, went over to the car he had leaned upon after killing Rizzato, and with the elbow of his topcoat carefully wiped his palm print from the fender.

Docker presented his ticket to the pimple-faced woman at the exit gate one floor above, entered the traffic stream which would take him up over the freeway and then down into the south-bound lanes. It was completely dark now, except for the blare of whizzing headlights.

"Somebody could be back there," Docker muttered aloud. He kicked it up to seventy-five, though the Millbrae exit he intended to take was only a long mile south, weaved through slower traffic as if with a release of terrific tension.

At the last possible moment, he jammed the wheel hard enough over so he screamed almost sideways right across three lanes of cars and whipped into the off-ramp in a yelp of scorching rubber and the thunder of serrated, crosswise warning curbs under his tires. Horns blared and brakes shrieked, but nobody hit him; and then the Montego was at a decorous exit-ramp twenty-five that would keep the CHP off its tail.

At El Camino Real, main artery of the Peninsula's tightly-packed suburban clutter, he went south again. Docker's fingers drummed the wheel. The mathmetical possibility of a tail still existed: somebody could have been behind him who had anticipated such an exit and had lain far enough back not to be caught napping.

Therefore, a squealing right into Trousdale from the left lane, in front of a station wagon being stood on its nose by its outraged woman driver. Left into Marco Polo, seconds later right into the spacious grounds of Peninsula Hospital, twist the wheel again to shoot into a DOCTORS ONLY slot in a small courtyard beyond the arched ambulance entrance, killing lights, motor, and sliding down in the seat all in one motion.

Nothing. No green Plymouth or any other car thrust a

questing nose into the courtyard; none passed in the blacktop beyond the arch.

Docker got out of there, for fifteen minutes played around in the curved residential streets lacing the subdivisions rising up the flank of the hills between Burlingame and the sea. Nobody stuck to his mirror for more than a block. Adeline Drive carried him into Hillside, and Hillside soon found the old Skyline which Interstate 280 had rendered obsolete.

Here Docker turned the big car north, back toward the city from which he just had escaped. Thirty feet short of a lonely phone booth, he pulled off on the shoulder. He got out a large flashlight, went over the car quickly and competently for electronic bleepers which might have been placed on the unguarded machine in the airport parking garage. It was clean, but Docker still seemed set on preparing for some final action; he got the long-armed lug wrench from the trunk and put it on the front seat beside the attaché case.

He limped to the phone booth, shut the door long enough to dial, then opened it so he would be in darkness. The car lights were off. He was only a shadow listening to the electronic bleeps and chuckles which would carry him through to his number. As he waited, he stared unseeingly at the great gleaming castles of the airport far below and a couple of miles away.

The operator asked for more money. Interstate 280 whined late commuter traffic south and early fun traffic north. Belatedly, Docker ripped a handkerchief apart with his teeth, stuffed enough of the strips into his mouth to give him the distinctively muffled voice which carried so much greater menace than normal tones ever could.

"Hariss residence." Young voice, female.

"Give me your father."

"Huh?"

Docker's tongue adjusted his mouthful of sodden linen. "Give me your father."

Careless clatter of receiver on Formica countertop. Steps receding, teen-age voice bawling. Steps returning.

Slight scrape of receiver being lifted. Abrupt rattle of another extension being picked up.

"Walter Hariss speaking."

"Get the cunt off the other line."

After a momentary silence, Hariss' voice, congested with rage, said, "Dawn."

"Bi-i-ig deal," said the teen-age voice. "I've heard it before." But within a few seconds, Docker and Hariss were alone on the line.

"Listen, you bastard, whoever you are, my family—"

"It's Peeler," whined Docker in his asthmatic voice. He became querulous. "His teeth are all over the floor. I had to wipe his blood off my shoes."

The silence was longer this time. Hariss' tense, almost frightened voice said, "Gus . . . Gus is . . ."

"His nose is up under his forehead." Docker's laughter almost got away into hysteria. "Marquez. Kolinski. Rizzato."

There was cold terror in the importer's voice by this time.

"Doc . . . Is this Docker? What do you want?" He was almost whispering. *"What is it,* damn you? You've got the . . . the merchandise, the money . . ."

The operator said, "Your three minutes are up, sir, please signal when through."

"Thank you, operator." Docker laughed again. "That's how long you've got, Hariss—as far as I am away from you. Then . . ."

"My God!" whispered Hariss' new, terrified voice. "Lo . . . look, you've got a quarter of a million in dope, street prices. Keep it. You've got a hundred-seventy-five thousand cash. Keep it. All—"

"I want your life, Hariss," said Docker in measured tones that carried conviction even through the muffling handkerchief.

"But . . . but *why?"*

Docker laughed again. The laughter went into registers where normal laughter never went.

"Does that matter, Hariss? Your life. Tonight."

The line was dead. Docker had hung up.

Twenty

Walter Hariss hung up the phone with a shaking hand. Sweat was running down his face. He looked around the ornate study with eyes whose whites showed all the way around the pupil, giving his heavy features a slightly owl-like look. The eyes did not seem to register what they were seeing. The shaking hand found a cut-glass whisky decanter, splashed generously into imported glass. Italian glass, hand-blown, $86.76 a dozen whole-sale . . .

The phone was ringing. Walter Hariss raised his head. He looked stupidly at the glass in his hand. It was emp-ty. The level in the decanter on the sideboard was three inches lower.

Panic flooded across his features. His eyes sought the Seth Thomas clock, a thing of chrome and plastic and gleaming brass on the antiqued oak sideboard.

Twelve minutes since Docker's call. Twelve precious minutes gone.

The phone was still ringing. Walter Hariss ran his hand over his eyes, across his fleshy face, as if attempt-ing to dismiss the nightmare.

The phone had stopped ringing.

His daughter's footsteps came to the study door. She called through the thick hardwood. "I said you were on the other line. He said he'd call back in five minutes."

"Who . . ." His voice had an odd tone. He stopped, adjusted it, as if to isolate his family from a viral conta-gion. He'd had an argument with Dawn on the way home, their relationship was still tender. "Who was it?"

"A man named Neil Fargo. He said—"

"Good! Thank you, Dawn." The name seemed to act

as adrenalin on him. Intelligence and cunning were once more moving behind his eyes. "If I'm on the other line when he calls, tell him to hang on. I want to speak with him. Don't let him hang up."

"I'll rape him," she said through the door in her sexiest tones.

He got out "Dawn!" sharply before recognizing the mockery in her voice. He finished lamely, "Whatever you think best, Dawn."

She went away. He dialled on the other line. After several rings, the voice of Blaney, the overweight Rock Hudson, answered, "Bush Street."

"Where's Daggert?"

"Out for hamburgers, Mr. Hariss."

"Want to start earning that percentage, Blaney? And there's fifty cash each in it for you and Daggert besides."

"You're on, Mr. Hariss."

"Good. Call in a couple of the temporaries, and then as soon as Daggert gets back, you and he come directly to my house, understand? Four-eighty-eight Sea Cliff Avenue, in the traffic circle right beyond Phalen State Beach parking lot."

Dimly, he heard the other phone ringing, heard his daughter's voice in the hallway, heard her step outside his door.

"Daddy . . ."

He turned from the phone. He called, "Right. Thanks, Dawn. I'll take it in a second." Back to the phone. Speaking with the strongarm, his voice had none of the fear it had carried in speaking with Docker. "Right away, Blaney, understand?"

"Got you, Mr. Hariss."

"I want both of you armed."

He hung up, picked up the other phone, hesitated momentarily as if he feared it might be another call from Docker; but when he spoke his voice was an executive snap. "Is that you, Fargo?"

"Me. Listen, I'm in a pay phone at the airport. All hell broke loose out here while I was sitting in the middle of a fucking traffic jam at South City. Docker's gone again. Still by car, not by plane. One of your inside men, some hippie kid, is in custody for trying to steal an attaché case—"

"Docker's?"

"You hired the kid, you know what you told him to do." Neil Fargo laughed without any particular mirth. "Your other man, that fat little guy dressed up like Robin Hood, was found in the elevator over in the parking garage, out cold. People found him thought he'd had a heart attack. but I saw him and there were some mighty big red marks on his neck. And some lady lost her lunch when she found Peeler stuffed under her car down in the lower level of the garage. So Docker's been around."

Hariss was having trouble with his voice again. "Gus . . . ah, had Gus been struck in the face?"

There was surprise in Neil Fargo's voice. "Yeah. Hit under the nose with a hard narrow object. The cops think it was the leaf out of an auto spring, but I know damned well Docker karate-chopped him—I've seen that fucker in action before. Peeler would have died of encephalitis from having bone driven up into his brain anyway, but he was D.O.A. when the cops got there. Which means he didn't make any dying statements, and you're still in the clear."

Hariss fought to keep the terror out of his voice. "In the clear? I'm not . . . not in the . . . Fargo, you've got to get up here! Docker called me. Here at home! He said—"

"I thought your lines were unlisted."

"I . . ." It was Hariss' turn for surprise. "They are! How . . ."

"Did Roberta Stayton know them?"

"Not from me," said Hariss.

"Kolinski?"

"Certainly."

"There's your answer. If she was planning on setting up you and Kolinski for some kind of fall, she'd have asked. What did Docker say?"

"He's . . . he said he was . . ." Hariss was striving for an offhand delivery, but his voice slid into a higher register in midsentence, like a teen-ager's. "Said he's coming to kill me. Do you think Roberta Stayton hired him to—"

"What difference does it make if he's on his way?" His voice had tightened and thinned. "Stay away from windows. Keep the blinds drawn. How long ago did he call?"

"Nearly . . ." Hariss checked the Seth Thomas again. "Nearly half an hour ago. But he was calling long distance. The operator said his three minutes were up."

Neil Fargo growled, "That doesn't mean a fucking thing, long distance starts at the San Mateo County line."

Hariss was reacting to Neil Fargo's reaction; the sweat was standing on his face again, and his fingers were slippery around the receiver.

"I've got Blaney and Daggert on their way out. Armed."

"He'll go through them like a maggot through shit." Neil Fargo's voice was almost bitter. Then his tone changed, lightened. "Still, maybe not. He's got a bum leg now he didn't have when I knew him in Nam, it's got to have slowed him down some. At least it'll limit the ways he can come at you. All right. Put Blaney on the front gate, Daggert on that point of rock out by your observatory . . ."

"Shouldn't somebody be inside?"

"You've got guns there, haven't you? Point one at the front door and pull the trigger if anything you don't recognize comes through it. Tell your strongarms to stop anything that moves. If it doesn't stop, shoot it. Tell them not to let Docker anywhere near them. I mean anywhere—not within three or four yards. I remember that son of a bitch once . . ."

He stopped. Hariss said, "What about you?"

"I'll be there as soon as I can. But the fucking fog has started to come in, that's going to slow traffic on the Bayshore. It'll probably take me an hour or better."

As he was talking, the sound of a doorbell came faintly through the closed study door. Panic surged into Hariss' voice. "There's . . . somebody at the front door, Fargo! Some . . ."

"That'll be your troops."

"What if it isn't?"

"I doubt if even Docker's got that much nerve. If you're worried, have your daughter answer it. He doesn't have a hard-on against her, does he?"

"I don't even know why he has one against me," said Hariss lamely.

"Go let in your troops." The detective laughed. "Let's *hope* it's your troops. Tell that fucking Blaney not to put a bullet in me when *I* show up. I'm on my way."

The fog Neil Fargo had mentioned had thickened, was rolling in from the sea through the Golden Gate, pouring white and silent up the natural passage of the bay and reaching thin greedy fingers out at the city. Alcatraz was blotted out, gone, as were the lights of Sausalito north in Marin County and the garlanded string of lights which marked Oakland, Berkeley and Richmond in the Eastbay.

In the city, especially in the Marina District which lay close to the water, it was wetting down the streets, haloing the headlights and streetlamps, muffling the sound of traffic and city night noises.

Neil Fargo was driving west on Lombard toward the Golden Gate Bridge approach through the mist-pastelled neons of U.S. 101's motel row.

He turned on his wipers and the defroster to keep the windshield clear, maneuvered his car into the left lane. This would allow him to stay on Lombard when the bridge traffic took an angle right into Richardson Avenue and then Doyle Drive and the bridge approaches. Lombard, suddenly narrow and tree-arched once it lost the bridge traffic, would take him to the Presidio Main Gate.

Through the Presidio was the shortest, most direct access to Twenty-Fifth Avenue, where the winding, rich, very private streets of Sea Cliff began.

Neil Fargo waited through the traffic to the green arrow, went across the in-bound lanes past the traffic islands. He had gone less than a block on this narrow, uncrowded Lombard before stopping the car. Across the street was a small bar splashing yellow light out into the fog. Directly ahead were the Presidio Main Gates, open and unguarded. Beyond them, Lombard became curving Lincoln Boulevard.

The detective had to wait for two cars to pass before he could trot across the narrow blacktop to the phone booth outside the bar. In the open air the mist was palpable, able to be felt on the face, between the fingers, in the nostrils. It was chill and fresh.

He shut the door so he could see to dial; the fog-dimmed corner street lamp was not enough. His fingers ticked off a familiar set of digits, five-five-three-oh-one-two-three. His face was absolutely icy.

"Police."

"Give me the radio room."

There was a series of clicks, a pause, then another voice—this one hard and male—came on with "Central Dispatch."

"Yeah, I want to report a stolen vehicle."

"You want the Auto Detail."

"This is hot," said Neil Fargo. "It'd better go out on the air right away. I'll shove the details to Auto later."

"Shoot."

"Nineteen-seventy-four Mercury Montego sedan license six-three-three, Zebra, Frank, Frank, color yellow. My name is Neil Fargo, that's F-a-r-g-o."

"You the registered on the vehicle?"

"Ah . . ." He had to consider his reply. "I'm the . . . ah . . . one who rented it. It was stolen by a man named Docker, that's D-o-c-k-"

"Docker, did you say?" The voice had been startled out of its habitual and professional phlegm.

"That's right, Docker. And you're right. You have him on an A.P.B., material witness on a homicide down on Bryant Street this A.M. You might not have it yet, but San Mateo's going to be putting him on the air in connection with the killing at the airport of—"

"Jesus! He in on that one too? The car's already going out on the air, Mr. Fargo. You got a vicinity where it was stolen?"

"Sixteen hundred block of Pine, that's Pine and Franklin, about ten minutes ago. I think he took off out Frank . . . Jesus Christ!"

From the phone booth window, Neil Fargo had been casually scanning traffic, the cars in and out of the Presidio, as he had been talking. Even in the couple of minutes he had been there, the fog had gotten thicker, heavier, an opaque blanket instead of rolling patches with clear spaces between. Visibility was down further yet, but the detective's face was suddenly crammed against the glass.

"The son of a bitch just drove by me!" he yelped into the phone. "Right by me in the goddam car!"

"What is your 10–20 . . . er . . . your location?"

"Oh! Lombard. Lombard and, ah, what the shit's the street at the Presidio ga—Lyon. That's it. He went through the Presidio gates!"

"We'll alert the Military Police as well as SFPD units," said the dispatcher. "And thanks, Mr. Fargo."

Neil Fargo hung up, stood in the booth for long moments, his head down as if in contemplation of unwelcome thoughts. Finally he opened the door. Through the fog, he could hear a police siren somewhere far off. Or, considering the fog, perhaps not so far off.

As if released from his regrets by the sound, he sprinted across the street toward his car, which he had left with the motor running and the wipers still snickering at the fog.

Twenty-One

The yellow Montego was blocked by three cars waiting at the stop sign where Lincoln and Presidio Boulevards rub noses. Docker, big hands steady on the wheel, face set in concentration, didn't even shift his foot off the accelerator. Instead, he goosed it.

And whipped into the left-hand lane on the wrong side of the miniscule triangular concrete traffic island, horn blaring to freeze traffic. He slewed across Presidio untouched because a sports car driver had damned good reflexes, fishtailed the rear end on fog-wet blacktop and was heading down Lincoln toward the old wooden building that had been Letterman Army Hospital until the new plant had been completed.

Behind him, the air was full of sirens. Directly ahead, an olive green Military Police jeep went into a skid of its own, broadside across the street to block his way, shedding MP's expecting the crash.

Docker jumped the left-hand curb, skun the left side of the Montego on the ancient stone retaining wall in front of some officer's white frame house, hit the blacktop still accelerating, fighting it under control with big, competent hands.

Ahead on his right behind masking palm trees, the greyish stucco cube which housed the MP Headquarters spilled men in Army greens and wearing white plastic helmet liners. They ran at the road drawing cumbersome Army-issue .45's. Docker aimed the Montego at the closest one, slewed away as the man dove back.

Men were on their bellies, squeezing off shots. One slug smashed against the post between the windshield and the frame on the far side of the car, but then the fog had closed in behind Docker again. His last mirrored view was of men sprinting toward a whippet-aerialled jeep.

The Presidio of San Francisco is an Army post, and has been in the hands of somebody's military since the Spaniard José Moraga erected an adobe stockade there in 1776. Since it has always been a defensive, not a training camp, relatively little of its total acreage has ever been in actual use. Most of its thousands of eucalyptus, monterey pine and cypress trees were planted by school children on Arbor Days in the early 1900's. Miles of earth and blacktop roads wander through these miniature forests.

But once pursuit had begun, the Presidio was not a particularly good place for Docker to be. It was a closed system; though the gates were always open, access could be controlled by sealing them up. Once inside, Docker had very limited options.

But he did have the fog. That was on his side.

On their side were their radios. Though Docker could not hear them, the air around him crackled with messages as he knifed the big car down the Lincoln Boulevard straight-away past the Parade Ground.

"Unit three, do you read me?"

"10–4, Control."

"Subject vehicle outbound on Lincoln. Vehicle is 10–99. Repeat, 10–99. Stolen vehicle."

"10–4, Control."

"Unit Seven, is the Broadway gate closed and locked?"

"Affirmative, Control. Am now sealing Presidio Boulevard gate at Pacific Street."

"10–4. Is any unit in the vicinity of MacDowell and Lincoln?"

"Affirmative. Unit Five en route that intersection on MacDowell. ETA, sixty seconds."

Ahead of Docker, Lincoln divided for an old red brick building which had been there much longer than the automobile and currently housed Army C.I.D. He slammed the brakes to set up a skid, goosed it as he came out of the slide, nose to the right, braked, jammed the wheel left. The rear end caromed off the springy steel guard-rail which divided Lincoln from a steep embankment below the Doyle Drive skyway to the Golden Gate Bridge.

He was still moving, but a tire was scraping something now.

The fog shifted momentarily; thirty yards off to Docker's right, serenely unconscious of it all, the freeway traffic whipped along, its many eyes fog-misted. The Mercury's headlights took ineffectual bites at the swirling mist as he roared along Lincoln. To his left, the National Cemetery's rows of honored dead under their simple markers marching up the hillside were invisible.

"Unit Five approaching MacDowell and Lincoln."

"10–4. Stop vehicle. Repeat, stop the vehicle. Subject is considered armed and dangerous. Subject may be heading for Crissi Airfield, over."

More sirens, they seemed to be coming from every compass point now, rising and falling as they cried to one another through the night. Docker's window was down so their voices poured in at him with the fog and the wet. He was hunched over the wheel like a race driver, his face, by the upthrust glow of the dash lights, was rendered less than human from intense concentration.

Ahead, intersection. MacDowell, leading down to Crissi Field. His hands did not twitch the wheel that way. Headlights on MacDowell in the fog.

"Subject vehicle approaching at high speed . . ."

The jeep leaped from the fog, trying to cut Docker off. But he was by MacDowell ahead of them with inches to spare. The jeep shot right across Lincoln, rammed headfirst into a tree.

"Unit Five, come in."

Docker heard only motor roar, saw only grey wetness, arc of his own lights.

"Unit Five, this is Control. What is your 10–20?"

"Bastard beat us to MacDowell. 10–51. Repeat, 10–51. Need a tow truck. No injuries."

"We do not read you, Unit Five. Did you make connection with subject vehicle, over?"

"We made connection with a tree, over."

"Unit Two, what is your 10–20?"

"Ruckman Avenue, heading for the underpass below U.S. One, over."

"Intercept—"

"Subject vehicle just passed intersection with Ruckman."

"Believe subject headed for Golden Gate Bridge access from view area. Can any unit block that intersection?"

Behind the wheel, Docker was laughing with apparent exhilaration. He shouted a snatch of song. He screamed through the stop sign where Crissi Avenue came up from the airfield below, shot a look down Crissi over his shoulder. Just fog.

"This is Unit Four. We are en route Golden Gate Bridge access from Lincoln Boulevard view area over Baker Beach. Will intercept subject vehicle."

"10–4. If subject attempts to run roadblock, initiate fire. Subject armed and dangerous."

Docker avoided the tempting trap of Marine Drive, which deadended at old Fort Point under the soaring red steel parapets of the bridge. Instead, he drifted the yellow car around the curved approach toward the intersection with the bridge view area. He had a momentary glimpse of yellow pinpricks on the Marin headlands hiding Sausalito, then the fog slammed the door shut, closing him back into its narrow dripping grey room.

"Control, this is Unit Four. Turn-off to View Area is a hundred yards ahead. No sight of subject veh . . . Headlights!"

"Detain vehicle, Unit Four."

The open window gave Docker the screaming sirens. Dim in the fog, a splash of light to mark the intersection. A hard right, a hard left, and he would have been aimed into the northbound lanes of the bridge. Northbound to Marin where a thousand suburban roads waited.

Headlights, glaring in his eyes. White flashes behind them whining bullets at him; none hitting.

Docker stood on the brakes. Docker put her into a skid, spinning the wheel hard.

But not going right. Going left. The nose tore through dirt, a rear fender wiped out a signpost bearing the words:

DEAD END. NO THOROUGHFARE

But he was into narrow Armistead Road, behind him the jeep went by like a hog on ice, all wheels locked uselessly as the MPs within raked the darkness into which Docker had disappeared with equally useless carbine fire.

Ahead, Y-junction. Left, Hoffman Street, dipping seductively downhill. No hesitation. Docker stayed on Armistead, accelerated as the street climbed between enlisted men's housing, past parked cars and the litter of the complex kids' toys only an affluent technological society can create. Up, all four wheels momentarily off the ground.

Crash! the car struck the blacktop, rocked. Barrier ahead. Flimsy wood, another crash, boards flew. Roaring down a steep grade, following the twisting street unerringly, braking, braking . . .

T-junction just below. Docker came to a full stop, lights out, just as an olive green MP sedan whipped by unseeing on Lincoln. Intentionally or not, Docker had come in a circle. Lights still out, he wrenched the wheel over, shot into line behind the MP vehicle, using their lights. Crissi angled in again like a bad summer rerun.

"This is Control. Where is subject vehicle?"

"Unit Four. Vehicle left Lincoln at Hoffman Street."

"Hoffman Street has a temporary wooden barricade across it. Block access . . ."

"What the hell!"

"Receiving your transmission poorly, Unit Four. 10–9 your message."

"Subject vehicle riding your lights, Unit One."

The olive green sedan with Docker tight behind had swung around Lincoln and back toward the view area access again. The sedan began bucking and sliding as it tried to stop where it could block the bridge access road. Instead, it slid right by and into the side of Unit Four, which was backing out of Hoffman Road like a frustrated foxhound from a blocked lair. No way by for Docker now, on Lincoln, to get out to Twenty-fifth Avenue.

Hard right, his lights transfixing gaping neckers, fishmouthed in the glare as he slewed by them. Across the access to the northbound bridge lanes was parked a CHP black-and-white, meticulously observing the Military Police's jurisdictional sway.

Docker didn't even try. Instead, he whipped a vicious left between concrete traffic islands stuffed her straight into the underpass which led beneath the toll plaza's multilanes.

Beyond the open square of tunnel, T-junction. Left again.

This put the fleeing Montego on a sunken access road that rose quickly up to highway level. Left again would put him on the return lanes to the city, inbound on U.S. 101.

But right . . .

Gunning forty, forty-five, fifty, right through the Bridge Employees Only parking lot. This was enclosed by a ten-foot high hurricane fence but at the far end was a wide double gate with a green sign reading "25th Ave. Exit."

Twenty-Fifth Avenue was where Sea Cliff began— Sea Cliff, where Walter Hariss lived.

A jeep was beside the gate, two uniformed MPs were in the act of running the two sides shut.

"*Hai!*" yelled Docker as if he were delivereing a karate blow.

His lights pinned them to the mesh. They leaped, for the instant movie stuntmen caught up with by real life, then they were tumbling away, skun-up but unhurt, as with a terrible spronging impact Docker's car hit the place where the two gates met.

Through, gates wide and drunkenly bent behind him, instantly gone in the fog. Lights probing great shadowy cypresses bent back away from the road, from the sea, by the incessant ocean winds.

By breasting the hill, Docker would find an intersection with Lincoln Boulevard which still might be able to carry him out of the Presidio at Twenty-Fifth Avenue.

But the big yellow car just kept going straight after it had gone through the gate. Off the reddish shoulder of the road, crash, thump, metal dragging the ground but still moving. Docker not decelerating, roaring along a narrow, rutted gravel and dirt road full of potholes that struck the springs like cannon fire. High beams here, where the fog was made patchy by crumbling concrete gun emplacements from World War II on the right, the backs of weathered clerical buildings of the same vintage with old-fashioned screen windows on the left.

For the moment Docker was totally lost to the pursuers behind. Fog like smoke, close-set cypresses, the gravel road suddenly three gravel roads, each of them also branching . . .

Hard shuddering turn to the right, gravel thundering on the car's underbody. Toward the ocean, losing options, trapped in a narrow strip of wild wasteland between sea-cliffs and Lincoln Boulevard. Scrub brush. Gnarled, wind-tortured cypresses. Somewhere behind, faint as baying hounds, the lights and sirens of pursuit.

Here, dripping fog. Brush. Then an opening out, a sense of breadth and distance. On his right, the immense grey bulk of an abandoned gun emplacement and bunkers pitted by the shell-fire of time.

Swirling fog sent his lights reflecting whitely back, but Docker could see he was on a huge flat gravel area nearly as large as a football field. He drove on, slowly now as if feeling his way.

The breadth narrowed. Great flat brow of bunker on the right, unbroken as a prison wall, pinching him left, left. Until ahead the wall ended in densely tangled brush no car could get through.

Wall on the right, impenetrable brush ahead, pursuit somewhere behind. And to the left, the gravel expanse just . . . ended.

Dead ended. The only way out was the way by which he had come in.

Docker backed the sleek, battered car away from the brush fifteen, twenty feet, paused, then turned left and drove very slowly forward toward the abrupt lip his lights showed him despite the great ropes of fog flowing up over the cliff face. He stopped a dozen feet from the edge of oblivion.

Docker left the lights on, the motor running, got out almost leisurely. He seemed to have all the time there was. Behind, somewhere, the ineluctable keen of sirens, but it was if these had lost all meaning and importance now.

He walked out beyond his headlights, stood with his feet on the crumbly edge of California. From directly in front and far below, three hundred feet below, came the startling blunt thud of breakers on jagged rock and hard wet sand. Thud, thunder of withdrawal, like distant, out-moded trains, thud again. Since the million years of rain which had cooled a spinning mass to make it the planet earth, it had been like that. And would be till the planet ceased to turn.

Darkness, death and thunder down below, pursuit and capture and another sort of death behind.

Docker walked almost idly back to the car, sat behind the wheel, leaving his door open for the moment. It could have been that the sirens were fractionally closer through the muffling fog. But sound plays tricks on dripping, misted nights.

Docker picked up the attaché case from the seat, got out, limped over to the brush with it. He opened it, by the glow of his parking lights stuffed into it his few small personal things; he would never need them again. Then he set the case in behind the twisted bushes where only someone with an idea of where to look would be likely to find it.

He went back to the car, got into it again. The sirens were definitely louder. There might have been a vague ghost of light cast momentarily up against the bottom of the fog somewhere behind him.

"Docker, baby, you've run out of time," he said aloud.

He picked up the lug wrench he had placed on the seat earlier, hefted it in his still-gloved hands as if momentarily considering it as a weapon.

But the lug wrench was not a weapon. The time for weapons was past. Docker snorted through his nose as if at his own hesitation.

He looked back once again. Aura of light, definite now. The sirens moaning closer, perhaps only seconds away. He turned and looked to his front, through the windshield that could show him only pouring fog. Docker's hands convulsed around the wheel.

Docker shifted his weight, and the accelerator was depressed, stayed down, the motor rose to a whine, a roar like a jet's run-up. Finally his hand hovered over the gear shift. The fingers flexed. The hand, with a convulsive movement, rammed it into low.

The Montego shot forward, Docker's final shout lost in the rattling spray of gravel against the undersides of the fenders as the rear wheels spun for traction. Slightly fish-tailing, the car shot out into the void. Its lights glared for a moment at the lip of gravel, then looked at only vertical fog as it dropped into space.

The first pursuing jeep, whippet-aerial slashing like a rider's crop, burst out onto the gravel field just as the Montego, somersaulting lazily in mid-air, struck the sharp granite shoulder which thrust far out into the sea three hundred feet below. The jeep slowed to a stop with its lights on the drag-strip wheel marks leading to infinity.

"What the hell . . ." the shocked driver had begun, when the car, far below, exploded.

The four men were out and running for the edge with the thump hitting their ears after the light of the blast had already dazzled their eyes. They stood in a clump, staring down at the fiercely burning wreckage. Despite the fog, it lit up the brown sand and the ugly black teeth around which the sea boiled in oddly delicate traceries of foam.

"Do you think he—"

"Yeah. He ran out of room," said the driver.

He looked back over his shoulder. The lieutenant was getting out of the sedan which had pulled up, slowly, as befits an officer. He had all the time he needed, neither car nor driver was going anywhere again. The lieutenant's watch didn't end until morning, he had nowhere else to go either. He was a young tight-ass black man.

With infinite leisure, the lieutenant sauntered over and looked down at the glowing mess on the rocks below, now scattered and burning through the mist in a dozen different places.

"Always some goddam thing," he said. He motioned to his driver. "Better call the fire department."

The man went away to work the radio.

"Alert the Coast Guard, too," the lieutenant called after him. "They'll want to send a patrol boat in from the ocean side."

After that, all they could do was watch it burn, and take turns wondering whether they really could smell the roasting flesh.

Twenty-Two

The weathered whitewashed building and miniature triangle of sand which comprise Phalen State Beach are open to the public, hence are unwelcome to the residents of the exclusive Sea Cliff area. But Phalen State Park has been there longer than many of them, and will probably outlast the rest of them. It is new money in Sea Cliff these days, *nouveau riche* money that thinks it has Arrived, but that is laughed at behind the discreet hands of Presidio Terrace money. San Francisco is an old and a cruel city, and one of the few that honors its bawdy past more than its supposedly progressive present.

At night, the gate which closes the winding walkway down to the public beach is closed and padlocked and the tatty little parking lot is indifferently lighted. Neil Fargo was just a dark, bulky shape crossing the lot. He shivered in the wet chill of the fog. His shoes scraped muffled shards of sound from the wet concrete. Somewhere below him in the mist, surf growled like a baffled tiger.

He had taken only about fifteen minutes longer than the hour he had estimated while talking with Hariss on the phone.

"Hold it right there, mister."

Neil Fargo stopped dead in his tracks. The flashlight struck him in the chest, stayed there while he very slowly brought his empty hands out of his topcoat pockets and spread his arms wide.

The light moved up to his face to identify him, blind

him for a few moments. and kill his night vision for twenty minutes. It dropped again. Nicely done. He could not see the figure behind the light. but it was probably Blaney. If it was, Blaney was probably holding the light at arm's length so a shot at the light would miss him. Just a strongarm, perhaps, but Blaney had managed to stay around for quite a few years. He was the only one of Kolinski's people that Fargo had ever even met. All the others were new, untried.

"Neil Fargo," said Neil Fargo.

"So it is."

Still the detective did not move. He was a dozen yards from the gate, electrically controlled, which was set flush on impenetrable hedges of Italian buckthorn.

"My piece is on the belt on the right-hand side."

Brisk, impersonal hands removed the weight from his hip, briefly patted him down for other armament.

"He sounded goddam jumpy on the phone," said Neil Fargo while the frisk was going on.

The big indistinct shape stepped back. Neil Fargo's .38 was in its left paw. "I'm goddam jumpy myself, out here in the fog."

"Only a few minutes more," he said cheerfully. "Docker's dead."

"Not such a fucking hotshot after all, huh? Well, it don't break my heart. I've earned my fucking fifty bucks. I'll let you through the gate."

He waited while Blaney found the concealed switch among the green waxy leaves of the buckthorn and activated it with a key. The white picket fence—backed with a ten-foot height of pipe-framed hurricane mesh— swung wide. This automatically lit up the driveway like a Cecil B. De Mille production. The drive was blacktop, flanked with more white rail fence right out of the Kentucky bluegrass country. The head-high, formally clipped hedges were privet here.

"Better not step off the drive, Mr. Fargo," said Blaney's apologetic voice behind him. "The alarms are set."

"Jesus Christ, when does World War III start?"

"I guess when you got it, you're scared shitless somebody's gonna take it away from you."

The house was a good sixty yards back from Sea Cliff Avenue, sixteen rooms with a gently-peaked and slate-shingled roof, set above the drive and garages on an artificial plateau which had been gouged from the rounded forehead of the bluff. Three-storied, immense living room windows on the ground floor which would look out across the neck of the Golden Gate at the incredible rocky sweep of Marin headlands when there was no concealing fog. A house from the twenties, when San Francisco land had not been valued by the square inch.

The wide marble stairway led to an inset porch and a massive hardwood door decorated with wrought iron. It was too much house for Hariss' current financial status; he had to be fighting the payments, had to have gotten it on the come.

Neil Fargo knuckled the bell; lights came on so he could be inspected. He looked off to his right, toward an angle of the house plunging off into the fog to form a two-story, narrow observatory which seemed to grow from the steep brown hill.

Somewhere out there would be Daggert, the second guard.

It was Hariss himself opening the door, displaying bravado.

"Ah, Fargo." Old-world gentility tonight. "Come in. You have news?"

"Some."

Beyond the tall door was a hallway; from his single previous time in the house, he knew that the immense formal living room lay to the right. A powder room where arriving guests could freshen up was to the left, with a small reception room complete with fireplace beyond that. This had its own small serving kitchen.

"You still keep the Courvoisier in the reception room?" asked Neil Fargo. He turned left, with Hariss behind. Over his shoulder, the detective added, "I thought your daughter would answer the door."

"She's angry with me, she's decided to sulk in her room."

Hariss headed toward the serving counter from the pantry as they entered the reception room. The presence of the guards seemed to have calmed him. None of his earlier hysteria remained in his voice.

"You cut her allowance to a hundred a week?"

Hariss snorted appreciatively, but said, "She wanted to go out on her motorcycle tonight with some of her friends. In this fog, and with Docker on the loose, I had to . . ."

"You can let her go."

The detective's eyes were on the older man's back. Hariss was pouring cognac from a cut-glass decanter; he stopped dead when Neil Fargo spoke. There was a subtle relaxation of the back muscles. He finished pouring.

"You *do* have news."

Neil Fargo sipped the Courvoisier, one of the few liquors it is a mortal sin to drink any way but straight. "Some good, some bad."

"I can use the good."

Neil Fargo leaned back in one of the leather chairs which, with a low table of ancient scarred and varnished oak, were the room's only furniture. His face was exhausted, drawn; he looked puffy around the waist as if out of condition. He hadn't bothered to remove his topcoat.

"Docker is dead. He went off the cliffs in the Presidio and down on the headland rocks the other side of Baker Beach. The car exploded."

Hariss looked up quickly. "There's no question that he actually died in the crash?"

"He couldn't have lived through it. I've got a police band on my car radio, I picked up the chase on the way up from the airport. I swung by. They were trying to scrape enough of him off the rocks to make an ident when I left. They'll be at it all night. The military police got onto him somehow as he was on his way through the Presidio—"

"Coming here." Hariss shivered as if a fire should have been laid in the fireplace. "To take my life."

"He took the high dive instead. Ran a couple of roadblocks." His eyes were remote. "I remember that guy when he was the coolest head around."

"Less than two miles from here when he died." Hariss

shuddered again. His earlier suave jauntiness had disappeared as if Docker's death had paradoxically made his threat more real. "If he had made it—"

"He'd have taken the Bobbsey Twins outside without breathing hard." Neil Fargo set his empty snifter aside and struggled from the leather chair's embrace. "He was a rough fucker when I soldiered with him. Funny. After he came home with the other POWs. he swore nobody'd ever put him in a cage again. Then he dies in a burning car. That powder room have a can in it?"

Hariss nodded, tossed off his cognac like bar whisky, poured another. Neil Fargo had found the light switch, had pulled the door shut behind him. There was a small table flanked with strips of vanity lights for repairing makeup. In front was a red plush bench. Neil Fargo regarded his image in the mirror. It looked peaked, but he made it wink at him.

Through the door came Hariss' raised and impatient voice. "You said there was some bad news. Fargo."

"Docker wasn't all that went over the cliff."

He took toilet paper from the roll; with it wound around his fingers he flipped up the seat of the toilet. He unzipped. began urinating.

"Meaning what?"

"Meaning the MPs searched the area where the car went over, and didn't find anything."

Before flushing, he lowered the seat again, removed the top of the tank, still with the toilet paper around his fingers. He looked inside. He nodded and set the top of the tank on the seat.

"Meaning the attaché case is gone," called Hariss heavily.

"And the heroin. And the money."

Neil Fargo worked very quickly, then rezipped his pants, drew in his belt the couple of extra notches, put back the lid of the toilet, opened the seat to drop in the toilet paper, flushed it using the back of a knuckle, opened the door with the end of his topcoat sleeve as he had done in closing it a couple of minutes earlier.

Hariss was waiting for him. "We have only your word for that, Fargo."

"I wasn't the one doing the search," he said mildly.

"I don't mean that. I mean there's a reasonable chance that you and Docker were in this together from the beginning. That he didn't have the money when he went to Bryant Street—"

"I wish you were right." He shot his cuff, checked his watch. "Because in just a little over twenty minutes I'm going to have to be convincing someone that his hundred-seventy-five thousand went up in smoke. I'd rather have the money to give back, believe me."

"You say. Meanwhile—"

"Meanwhile, you haven't come out so fucking bad, Hariss! So you're out the twelve, thirteen thou you paid for the smack in Mexico, and Kolinski is in the can and Roberta Stayton isn't around anymore to give you a lever to use on her old man. But you're out of jail, and you're clean. Nobody can tie you into anything."

Hariss snorted and turned away. Neil Fargo's hand darted out, scooped up the snifter he had drunk from, and dropped it into a topcoat pocket.

To Hariss' back, he said, "Well, do we keep on doing business together or is this going to scare you off?"

"I don't scare easy." The importer jabbed a finger into Neil Fargo's rock-hard gut. "But you brought Docker in—"

"And now Docker is out. All the way out. So you can *afford* to not scare easy."

The big detective went down the hall, stepped out under the miniature porte-cochere. He turned back toward Hariss, the overhead lights making his face very hard and momentarily quite nasty.

"I'll be in touch." His expression made it seem more threat than promise.

The fog seemed to have lessened. He waited while Blaney electronically swung the gate open again, collected his revolver and the handful of copper-jacketed bullets which had been in the gun when he had handed it to the strongarm.

"That's a nice piece, Mr. Fargo. Nice balance."

"Yeah. You're not too bad at being careful yourself, are you?"

"Man's gotta stay alive, Mr. Fargo."

"Might remember that if people start asking questions, Blaney."

Neil Fargo dropped the shells into one topcoat pocket, the gun into the other, tapped Blaney on the arm with a closed fist, sauntered off into the fog. Out of sight of the gate, he looked straight up and caught the veiled glow of a quarter moon. The fog was lifting.

At a clump of tightly-trimmed decorative bushes on somebody's lawn, he retrieved the attaché case he had found in the bushes above Baker Beach where Docker had left it. Ten fast minutes brought him out of the opulent residential area on El Camino del Mar. He walked in Lake Street to Twenty-Fifth, scattered dimes on the tray in a gas station phone booth on the corner of California, and started phoning.

His first call brought a familiar age-quavered voice. He said: "Jimmy? Neil Fargo."

"How'd I do, Mr. Fargo?"

"Beautiful. The timing was perfect on every call."

"That's great, Mr. Fargo. Makes me feel . . . Well, it's the next best thing to having my eyes back, to know—"

"There'll be a hun bonus, Jimmy."

"A hundred bucks? Mr. Fargo—"

"Everybody gets healthy on this one, Jimmy."

His next call was for a taxicab. He gave them the name of Smith and said he'd be waiting in the Lone Star Bar on Twenty-Fifth and Clement.

He checked his watch. Not yet ten o'clock. Events had moved very rapidly. He dialled, was rewarded with a sing-song voice speaking the name of a karate studio.

"Yes, Mr. Fargo, Mr. Tekawa wait for your call even though we all close up now. Here . . ."

"Okay, Hank, I just got the word. No. *After* I found out Kolinski O.D.'d the Stayton woman. Huh? Yeah, that's right. Anonymous, even within your own department. Shit, Hank, dummy up some paper leads to make it look like you dug it out of the woodwork yourself . . ."

He listened, nodded, grunted, shook his head, finally cut in again.

"Okay, you've got the judge lined up. You'll have him by the ass but he'll have good lawyers and . . . yeah. Okay."

He listened a final time, laughed.

"Thank me when you find out if the tip was any good or not. Hell yes, bring your partner in on the bust if you want. Just don't tell him the tip came from me." He recited a phone number from memory. "I'll be there for an hour or so. Let me know how it goes."

He walked the block to Clement, was standing in front of the little neighborhood bar when his taxi arrived.

Twenty-Three

The taxi driver didn't like hippie freaks and he didn't like coffee. He drank milk from a half-pint box on the dashboard as he drove.

"Night work like this, y'know, you gotta drink something. When I drank coffee I had this backache all the time. Got so bad I went to this doctor, see?"

Neil Fargo grunted. The fog was dissipating. He could see several blocks down deserted California Street.

"So he tells me I got something with a long name, see, and I should quit hackin'. So what'm I gonna do, sell apples?"

He shot a quick look at Neil Fargo to see how these confessions were being handled. He was short and middle-aged and wore a cardigan sweater bunched up around his upper arms.

"So I'd read this article somewheres about coffee, all the crap it puts in your blood stream, see, so I stayed hackin' but started drinking milk instead. You know what happened?"

"You don't mean to tell me," said Neil Fargo. "Next corner."

"That's right. My back quit aching, and that's like six, almost seven months ago." He pulled over to the curb, turned again to watch Neil Fargo getting out some money. "You can say what you want about them fuckin' hippies, but they got something in all this natural foods shit, y'know what I mean?"

Neil Fargo paid, tipped enough but not so much he'd be remembered. He was three blocks from his office. He said, "I think you've got something too. About milk."

The cabbie's face seamed in a grin. "Me an' Mark Spitz."

Neil Fargo walked down to the closed Seventy-Six station, got his Fairlane started so the defroster would clear the windows, left it running while he used the pay phone.

"I'm on my way up," he said. "Ten minutes."

California Street in-town was mostly clear of traffic apart from clots at the red lights and pedestrian crosstraffic where Grant Avenue dragged Chinatown athwart his bow. The fog had dissipated enough to show him the flat glitter of Treasure Island as he went down Nob Hill past a rattling, nearly-empty cable car. There was an empty slot across from darkened Tadich's Grill.

He walked back to Montgomery Street, and the two short blocks out to Clay where the immense leg-like white pillars slanted up to support the massive pyramid shape. He signed in with a fictitious name, for the second time that day was whisked up to Stayton Enterprises. The outer door past Miss Laurence's deserted desk was open, and Maxwell Stayton's blocky silhouette filled his private doorway.

Only when he turned to accompany Neil Fargo into his office did the lights slant across his features, showing how the day had ravaged them. But he said, "More like eighteen minutes."

"And time is money. How's Dorothy taking it?"

"Another fucking stupid question. Cognac?"

"No, thanks. I've already had one. Which reminds me."

He took the brandy snifter from his pocket which he had carried away from Hariss' house. Stayton frowned uncomprehendingly at it.

"Evidence?" he asked.

Neil Fargo nodded. He went around behind the desk. "Fingerprints?"

He nodded again, rapped the glass sharply on the rim of the wastebasket to break it, dropped the shards into the basket. "My own. I didn't want to leave any hard evidence I'd been out at Walter Hariss' house tonight, so I carried it away with me. If he can't prove I was there, he takes a long fall."

Maxwell Stayton began, "If you think I'm going to—"

"I came in with you, Max, remember? After we'd had supper together to discuss your daughter's murder. You pick the restaurant—somewhere they won't contradict anything you say. And have a word or two with the security guard here in case he's ever questioned—"

"Why should I?"

Neil Fargo sat down in the same chair as that morning. Also like the morning, Stayton sat down behind the desk. The detective put his head back against the curved leather back, stared at the ceiling. His legs were thrust out ahead of him in utter relaxation, his hands hung loosely on either side of the chair arms. He was so motionless he might have been asleep.

To the ceiling, he said, "Because if you don't, the frame against Harris won't stick. Or *might* not stick. Of course you can tell me to go to hell. What the fuck, nobody pushes old Maxy Stayton around."

Stayton reached for a cigar. His hands shook, very slightly; it had been a long day. He said icily, "You'd do well to remember that, Fargo. With my daughter dead, your claim to my consideration . . ."

Neil Fargo met his eyes steadily.

"Uh-uh. I'll get by. You said this morning that you wanted the men responsible for Robin destroyed. And like magic, by tonight they're destroyed. I hope you like it."

"Kolinski destroyed himself by murdering Robin. As for Hariss—"

"Bullshit. Robin suicided. With ninety-five percent pure heroin that I used your hundred-seventy-five grand as bait to bring up across the border from Mexico."

Maxwell Stayton got almost clumsily to his feet and came around the end of the desk. His cigar was in his left hand. He slowly hooked a hip over the edge of his desk and leaned forward so he loomed over the younger man. Neil Fargo made no move at all.

"Say that again."

"Not that I knew Robin was going to get her hands on any of it," continued Neil Fargo as if the older man had not moved or spoken. "That was something she and Docker cooked up between them."

"Docker's the man you said this morning you trusted and shouldn't have? The same Docker who the eleven o'clock news said went off a cliff in the Presidio in a stolen car?"

"The same Docker."

Stayton said in a terrible, soft voice, "How did Docker and my daughter come to meet?"

"It's a long story. But he was in my employ, and—"

Stayton's heavy features convulsed. Without the rest of his body moving, his right arm swept in a tight vicious arc so his massive right fist smashed against Neil Fargo's cheekbone, driving his head sideways with such power that it upset him, chair and all. He hit the floor on one shoulder, came up with fists like rocks hanging at his sides, very much like a downed fighter will bounce up before the mandatory eight count to show he hasn't been hurt by the blow which floored him.

For quite thirty seconds, Neil Fargo stood in the middle of the room breathing deeply, staring at his employer with eyes like hot coals. Then the tension went out of his pose.

"Feel better?" he asked.

Stayton made a vague gesture. He went back around his desk, sat down slowly in the massive executive chair, slowly put his head between his hands. His cigar jutted out from between his palms like the barrel of a gun.

"When I said this morning I wanted them destroyed . . ."

"Roberta did it for you. At least Kolinski. She bought his destruction with her own death and with five thousand dollars for the testimony of the black girl on the desk."

Stayton's voice said brokenly from between his hands, "The five thousand for the black girl. That came from my hundred-seventy-five—"

"Yeah. Docker took it out at Robin's suggestion. I didn't even know it was missing until too late."

"It's . . . gotten away from me, hasn't it?" asked Stayton almost querulously.

"Yeah." Neil Fargo rubbed a palm across his bruised face. "You're past it, daddy. But you still pack a hell of a wallop." He suddenly shrugged wryly. "Shit, it got away from both of us."

A gleam appeared in Stayton's eyes. "Meaning Docker?"

"Docker and Robin. I should have been able to foresee that if she'd gotten sick of life she'd do something about it. *And* find somebody like Docker to help her do it."

He righted the chair he had been sitting in, slumped back against it once more. He tilted his head back, began talking in a soft voice.

"Let me tell you about Docker. Captain in my outfit in Nam, a tough cookie, the hardest man I've ever known. Then he was MIA, presumed dead until the big POW release, when he turned up on one of the lists. He looked me up when he came through Travis Air Force Base. Still just as tough, but the Cong had put him in a cage for a number of months. It turned the hard into nasty . . ."

He stopped talking. Stayton said, "Did Robin buy his cooperation, too?"

"They met in Mexico City," said Neil Fargo. He sighed and lowered his head to look at the industrialist. "That's where it got away from me. When you hired me to find Roberta this last time, and I found out here and in Mexico what I was up against—her addiction—and who I was up against—Kolinski and Hariss—I needed a wrecker. The Cong had made a wrecker out of Docker, so I contacted him in Vegas, where he'd gone to work as security in one of the big hotels, and hired him. Without knowing he and Robin had met in Mexico when she was down there trying to kick her habit, and had . . . I guess, had fallen for each other for a while."

"Why did you need a wrecker?" asked Stayton. "I gave you all the money you asked for . . ."

"Money wouldn't buy them off. Hariss wanted power —the sort of power you have—and Kolinski wanted Robin's degradation. *And* a drug distribution setup. They were bringing in a kilo of pure heroin; I made them think I had a cash buyer. *Your* cash, of course. Since I knew Hariss had an almost pathological fear of being himself involved in anything shady, I suggested Docker as bagman. That way, I said, none of the rest of us would have to show in it at all. Mexican courier, bagman, chemist, nobody else. Harris loved it. Kolinski was ouchy but he went along."

"So what went wrong?"

"*Docker* went wrong—the one element in the situation I thought was stable. He was supposed to lay out the courier and grab the heroin before the chemist showed up. Instead, he *killed* the fucking courier, hung around to beat up the chemist, then went on the run from me as well as from Kolinski's people. I thought he'd gone berserk. Now I know he was working to a pre-existent scheme he and Robin had worked out to destroy Kolinski."

"From the way he died, I'd say he intended to keep both the heroin and the money, and—"

"Not the money. I had never given him that, although he'd handled it, of course. Then this afternoon—"

The phone shrilled, cutting him off.

"That'll be for me," he said.

Neil Fargo crossed to the instrument, picked it up, said, "Yeah," and started listening. He listened for a full three minutes, interjecting only occasional monosyllables. He hung up. He seemed suddenly to dominate the room with ill-concealed excitement.

"They nailed that fucker," he said.

"Which fucker?"

"Walter Hariss. The narcs, on a tip and with a valid search warrant, just raided his place out in Sea Cliff. Taped to the inside of a toilet lid—the oldest gag in the book—they found a key of pure heroin wrapped in waterproof plastic. Stupid of Hariss, huh? But then the most careful guy around can be made to look stupid if he's worried about dying."

Understanding had dawned in Stayton's eyes. "You mean that you—"

"I mean that when the police technicians get busy inside those layers of plastic, they're going to find a lot of fingerprints from Julio Marquez, the courier who Docker killed this morning."

"And on the outside?"

"Smudges only, made by someone careful not to leave fingerprints."

"But careless enough to hide it inside the toilet tank?" Stayton was on his feet, prowling the office. The fog was gone, black night sky now cloudless, the twinkling insignificant carpet of San Francisco lights spread below his aerie. Facing the window, he said, "Are you really naive enough to believe they'll make it stick? With the sort of lawyers he'll be able to afford?"

"Hank Tekawa, the lieutenant in charge of the raid, is a hell of a bright cop," said Neil Fargo. "Besides, even if he beats this rap, Hariss won't be out of the woods."

Stayton whirled suddenly, pointed a blunt finger at him.

"I thought Docker was on the run with that heroin. How did you get it?"

"At one point he ran to the airport. I found him there, as did Kolinski's people. They didn't make it stick. Docker told me he was going to make a run for it, by car, to Marin County. I told him we had a chance to knock off Hariss, too, if he'd stop at a phone booth to call Hariss and threaten his life. Then Hariss would *ask* me to come to his house—to protect him."

"And Docker did it for you? And gave you the heroin? Just like that?"

"He and I went through a lot together in Vietnam. And he really didn't much give a shit any more whether he lived or died. Not once Roberta was gone. He left the heroin where he knew I'd find it once he saw he wasn't going to make it out of San Francisco."

Stayton sighed. "I'm not saying I believe you. But even if I did, your reconstruction leaves out one important item: my hundred-seventy-five thousand dollars. If Docker never did have it—"

"Hundred-seventy. Five thousand went to the black girl."

"All right. Hundred-seventy thousand."

"It's in a safe deposit box."

"In your name, I suppose?" There was a sneer in his voice.

"In Walter Hariss'."

There was a moment of frozen silence. Stayton exploded, "Are you mad? Putting that kind of money in—"

"Internal Revenue will receive the tip in the morning. One of the safe deposit keys will be found in Hariss' office desk. I put it there myself earlier this week. I dropped the other down a manhole this morning after putting the money in the box."

"But the signature won't be Hariss'—"

"He's going to convince Internal Revenue of that? A hundred-seventy-thousand in cash, old bills, not sequential, not traceable, not reported on his income tax returns? They'll pick him clean and jug him for tax fraud, then audit him for the rest of his life—even if he *would* beat the narcotics rap, which I don't believe for a second. The beauty of it is, however loud he screams, nobody'll believe it's a frame. The amount is just too goddam big. Nobody would put out that kind of money to do somebody down. That's why it'll work."

Stayton was silent for a time, mouth set in an angry slash. Finally he said, "And his family? His wife and daughter?"

"He should have thought of them before he started fucking around with Kolinski. You should have thought of them before you hired me."

Stayton had an expression in his eyes which could have been respect not unmingled with fear. "You're a cold-blooded bastard, aren't you, Fargo?"

"I'm a manhunter. I work at it."

"And you say that your friend Docker was a hard man?"

"Not hard enough," said Neil Fargo. "He's dead."

"So is my daughter."

"By her own hand, Stayton. Remember that. She wanted to die. She was a syphed-up junkie whore, she'd have died before she was forty of malnutrition or an accidental O.D. or one of the diseases hypes don't have enough resistance to avoid getting. Serum hepatitis, spinal meningitis—shit, you know the litany. This way she went out clean, took Kolinski with her—the man who'd made her what she'd become. Or at least had given her the opportunity."

Stayton looked old, crumpled, scarcely strong enough to have made the already discoloring bruise on Neil Fargo's face. "I'd better get home. The boy doesn't know about his mother's death yet, I haven't . . ." He stopped speaking. A frown creased his tired features. "You said your friend Docker was going to try to bust out—north, into Marin County. Why did he have to bust out? The police didn't know where he was or what he was driving. Only one man knew . . ."

Neil Fargo was silent for long moments. Then he nodded.

"Yeah. Sure. He could have pointed the finger at us all. At you. At me. He could have cleared Kolinski, could have cleared Hariss. And he had become an unstable man."

"But . . . he was supposed to be your friend! You . . . he'd saved your life in Vietnam."

Neil Fargo shrugged. "So I'm a son of a bitch. But I'm still alive. And Docker isn't."

"You won't ever work for me again, Fargo," the industrialist choked out. His voice shook. "You know that I value personal loyalty above any . . . Not now, not ever again."

Neil Fargo shrugged. From the doorway, he said, "You never gave a shit about what happened to Robin, Stayton. Only about the fact that she was carrying your name. You *think* you care she's dead, but you don't.

Not really. Now you've got her son all to yourself. You failed with her, you think you won't fuck it up this time with the kid. The only one who cared about Robin—*really* cared about Robin—was Docker. He loved her enough to help her go out with dignity."

The whey-faced financier said nothing. Neil Fargo nodded.

"My secretary will send you a closing bill and our final report in the morning."

He left. Back at his own office, he dictated the promised report, drinking bourbon straight from a pint bottle between paragraphs. When he'd drunk enough of it, he went to sleep on the office couch.

Twenty-Four

It was a mild morning. Pamela Gardner had her cloth coat over her arm when she paused in the vestibule of the street level door bearing the inscription NEIL FARGO—INVESTIGATIONS. She was humming a tune to herself with youthful resiliency, as if yesterday had not happened, or had happened to one of the characters in the weighty best-seller she again bore under her arm.

The office smelled of stale cigarette smoke. On the top step she stopped so abruptly that she dropped the book again, as she had done the morning before.

"Oh!" she exclaimed. "Oh! I . . ."

Neil Fargo turned from the electric coffee maker. He was scowling. "How the hell do you make this bastard thing work?"

"Oh." She was blushing, as if meeting him here before office hours made it an assignation rather than a work day. "You . . . have to jiggle the cord in the socket a certain way to—"

"Jiggle it," commanded Neil Fargo.

Pamela eyed the pot critically, did things with the cord no manufacturer's instructions ever included. The pot began to perk, hesitantly, like a two-cycle engine with only one cylinder working.

"You look hung over," she said snidely to the detective.

"I am. There's a report on the tape."

His hands had tremored ever so slightly while fooling with the coffee pot. His eyes were bloodshot. He had shaved with the office razor, but carelessly. He turned toward his inner sanctum.

"At least the janitor got the mess cleaned up last night. A cup of that when it's ready will save my life, doll."

But Pamela had followed him into his office. She laid the newspaper, folded open to the story, on the desk under his eyes. "Is that the same Docker?"

"The very same." His voice was mocking, but his eyes were somber.

"It says they haven't found the body yet, but that—"

"Yeah. He's dead."

The words were blunt. The girl's very small, very soft capable hands that smelled of Jergen's Lotion found another news story. "It says that terrible man, that one you called Peeler—"

"Yeah, he's dead, too." He added cruelly, "Virgins will now sleep soundly in their beds." She began to color. He said, "Roberta Stayton is dead. Julio Marquez is dead. They're all dead."

"Roberta Stayton made the front page." There was no sorrow in the small girl's voice. Her nose twitched, somewhat like a rabbit's. Her voice had been just short of snide.

"Her old man has the money, what do you expect? Which reminds me. Once that report is typed up, send him the original and our closing bill. Jack the price up —way up. We won't be shaking that particular money tree any more."

Her face was shocked. "Oh, Neil! He's our . . . he . . ."

"We'll just have to go back to doing legal investigations, doll." He laughed shortly, with little real pleasure. "Maybe we ought to offer our services to Walter Hariss. He's going to be needing a lot of help."

"Do you think they'll really make it stick?"

"It'll stick," he said solemnly. "But let's help it along. Give Internal Revenue a call, you're a secretary used to work for Hariss Ltd. down on Battery Street. You know for a fact he has a safe deposit box stuffed with undeclared cash. They'll take it from there."

Her eyes shone. "Oh, Neil, *does* he?"

"He does. I found it out just yesterday. I wasn't spinning my wheels *all* day."

"Why don't we claim the informant's percentage?"

"This one's for sweet charity, doll. Isn't that damned coffee ready yet?"

She disappeared, but no coffee appeared. Instead, he could hear the rattle of her electric typewriter. He seemed to forget about the coffee, merely sat behind the desk staring almost vacantly out the window. Pamela came back in, sat down on the edge of his desk closest to him. In that position she showed a dangerous amount of slightly chubby thigh; but there was a dangerous look in her eyes to match the display. Neil Fargo regarded the exposed flesh.

"What would your mother say?"

She started to blush, but she made no move to cover her legs and refused to lower her eyes from his. "I'd get an apartment of my own if I thought it would do me any good."

"It wouldn't."

"I know that, too. Neil, this report to Stayton—it's full of a lot of . . . of things that didn't happen."

"Such as?"

"Going down to Mexico to look for Roberta. You never went to Mexico. You told me three weeks ago, the day after Stayton hired us, that you thought she was right here in the city in a Tenderloin—"

"Jacks the expenses up," he said lightly.

"Can you tell me what really happened yesterday, Neil?"

"Part of it, doll."

He told her part of it, picking and choosing through

what had actually transpired. When he finished, her eyes were round.

"You took the heroin into Hariss' house stuffed down the front of your shirt? That man searched you . . ."

"Just a standard frisk for a gun—there wasn't much chance he'd find it."

"And . . . and Docker killed them both with his bare hands?"

"Self-defense, both times, but nobody would have believed it. Not the cops or the D.A., anyway—the ones who'd matter if it came down to arrest and trial."

"A jury would have believed him."

Neil Fargo shook his head slowly. "Remember, the Viet Cong had him for over a year before the North Vietnamese got him. He told me nobody'd ever put him in a cage again—not for one day, not for one hour. He said he'd kill his ass first."

Her eyes were shinning again. They were very blue, very clear. "He must have been a very brave man."

"Some Frenchman in the underground in World War Two said that only an optimist kills himself. How about that coffee *now*?"

She slid off the desktop reluctantly, started out with the back of her short blue skirt deeply creased from the hard surface. Then she turned back and stood in the doorway, with her crossed arms pushing her swelling youthful breasts together as if offering them for his approval.

"He loved her very deeply, didn't he? Docker?"

"I didn't get a chance to ask him, doll. Coffee."

She was in the outer office when the phone rang. She answered, after a few seconds laid down the receiver. Her heels detoured to the coffee pot before coming across the floor to his open doorway. She set down a steaming mug. Her face was tight.

"It's that Rhoda Walström who used to—"

"Thanks, doll." His briefing had not included Rhoda. He said into the phone, "Hello, darling, I was going to call you this morning. You at work already? Mm-hmm. Early, huh? Yeah, me too. The police been around yet?"

He winked at Pamela Gardner. She left abruptly, but he could hear her heels falter, stop within earshot. Sunshine slanting through the east windows laid her shadow on the floor near his office door.

"Wylie himself?" he said into the phone. "I'll bet he gnashed his teeth when you said . . ." He listened. He laughed. "I doubt if you really mind about ruined reputations, Rhoda. Tonight? Why not? I told Wylie you were a terrific lay, I guess I'd better make sure I didn't lie to the police . . ."

When he hung up thirty seconds later, Pamela's shadow was gone from the floor. He could hear her making secretarial noises at her desk. He checked his watch like a man marking time to an important appointment; his face was cold and withdrawn and totally without the animation he had injected into his chatter with the big Scandinavian girl.

The phone rang. A few moments later, Pamela called, "Neil. It's Inspector Wylie on line one."

He punched the phone off the HOLD she'd put it on, said, "Fargo" into it.

"I've been talking with Hank Tekawa this morning, Fargo," said the policeman's flat, impolite tones. "That was a lovely drug bust he and Maley made last night out in Sea Cliff. Apparently developed their whole case themselves through careful investigative blah blah bullshit."

"Give Lieutenant Tekawa my regards," said Neil Fargo. "Now, if there's nothing else, I've got an appointment in—"

"Thing is, Fargo, Hariss opened up like an oyster before his lawyer got there to shut him up. Claimed a frame engineered by you and this fellow who drove off the cliff at Baker Beach last night. Docker. Said Docker and you were in the same outfit in Vietnam, that Docker saved your life once, was a POW—"

"I doubt if Hariss' heroin-possession jury is going to give much of a shit about my war reminiscences."

"I do. You told me yesterday you didn't know Docker, at a time I had out a material-witness want on him in connection with a death by violence. Obstructing justice at least, maybe accessory after—"

"Did Hariss let it drop that the Docker in my outfit in Nam was MIA—missing in action? That he never turned up on any of the repatriation lists? That he is presumed dead by the military authorities?"

There was a long silence. Finally Wylie growled, "Are you just blowing smoke, or—"

"Walt Hariss isn't a very reliable witness, Inspector. I suggest that you check with the Army Records Center. See if you can find any of my prints out at the Hariss house. Find some witnesses that put me there last night. Then check with Maxwell Stayton on whether I had supper with him and went up to his office afterwards to talk about his daughter's murder. If you have any questions after all that, you've got my office phone number."

He hung up. His coffee was cold. He got out a cigarette, sat with it in his hands, his face almost stupid in its total lack of expression. He looked at the cigarette as if seeing it for the first time, stuck it unlighted back in his pack. He turned the page on his calendar. Then he rubbed his face with his hands, like a man who is worn out from overwork or insomnia.

He looked at his watch. Five to nine. He stood up so abruptly that he tipped over the empty wastebasket. He went out into the main office. His features were animated.

"I've got an appointment, doll."

She said in a small voice, "Neil."

He stopped and looked at her. "Well?"

"If . . . Docker didn't meet her down in Mexico like you said in that report, then where did he meet her?"

"Docker was a Bay Area boy originally, doll. Went with her in college for a while—like that. So when he came back from the Vietnam prison camp, I guess he looked her up. That's my reconstruction, anyway. And found her hooked on heroin. He must have felt something for her, because he let her drag him into her crazy scheme of revenge . . ."

"Oh." She said it in that small, distant voice. After a

long time she said, looking at her desk, "You turned him in, didn't you, Neil?"

"He killed two people."

"You . . . said it was self-defense both times."

He nodded. "Let's just say I knew he couldn't get away with it anyway, and that he was better off dead than in prison. If you don't like that, just say that I felt it was part of my job as a detective."

"That makes it a . . . pretty rotten sort of job, doesn't it, Neil?"

"Lots of people think so." He suddenly grinned. "It's the only one I've got." The grin faded. "If you're going to quit, Pam, make yourself out a check for a month's severance pay. I'll sign it when I get back. Now, I've got an appointment."

"I didn't say I was going . . ." But her voice trailed off.

"Up to you, doll. But you're not going to change me. And you're not going to change the job."

He went down the stairs quickly, wooden-faced, waved through the window at the Chinese woman who ran the beauty shop. She waved back, with a reminiscent smile. The smile was brilliant and quite alluring.

At the Seventy-Six station, Emil was waiting. Down in the next block the big yellow scavenger's truck grunted as one of the garbagemen pulled the lever which made it swallow up the trash they'd been dumping into its open maw.

"Hey, Fargo! What happen to big yellow car, huh?"

"Maybe Doc Follmer's compact ate it."

Emil grinned crookedly. He had very bad teeth. "Ha! Next time I charge you." He added in his atrocious accent, "That's nice car, you want sell to me?"

"Too late, Emil. It was stolen last night."

The Hungarian looked at him blankly for several seconds, then convulsed with laughter. "Is stole! Is stole off big private eye? I notice about five, six o'clock is gone, I think you take it. Instead, is stole!" He slapped his knee with delight.

Neil Fargo shrugged sullenly, from his car got a brown attaché case. He turned toward the men's room, paused, said, "It was a rental job, the insurance'll cover the replacement. Whoever took it sent it over a cliff out in the Presidio. Wedged down the accelerator with a lug wrench, stood outside the window and flipped it into low . . ."

"Is bad thing to do to nice car."

The detective went by the voluble Hungarian without answering, and went into the men's room. The single stall was closed; the restroom was cold and smelled of disinfectant. From outside, a door or two away, came the rattle of garbage pails as the scavengers emptied them into the hulking compressor truck.

Neil Fargo hoisted the attaché case up on the square white porcelain sink, unsnapped the catches. He opened it, stared at the contents. Then, belatedly, he put his fingertips against the closed stall door and pushed it wide.

"Hello, Docker," he said.

But the stall was quite empty.

He laughed thinly through his teeth, a sound almost totally devoid of mirth. He dropped something on the floor, trod it under his heel. It was a pair of horn-rimmed glasses with clear glass in the frames. He picked up the bent frames and dropped them into the big refuse pail the garbagemen would collect within a minute.

He lifted out the long ash-blond wig, and stuffed that down among the morning's wet, used paper towels. He made sure it was covered, so the scavengers for whose arrival he had been waiting would destroy it without even seeing it. He closed the attaché case.

"Goodbye, Docker," he said aloud.

His tone was somewhat like the tone he had used the previous day, in bidding goodbye to a junkie whore named Robin whom he had once loved very deeply. Deeply enough to give her those few moments of regained humanity before she slipped through the wall.

Neil Fargo heard the voices of the garbagemen, exchanging cheery profanities with Emil. He walked out of the cold little cubicle into the empty California sunshine, moving like a professional athlete the day after his team has lost the playoff game. The purple bruise Maxwell

Stayton's fist had left on his cheekbone only heightened the illusion.

Then he straightened slightly, as if about to pass a reviewing stand, pointed a forefinger at Emil as if it were a gun, moved his thumb twice to make the gun go bang bang, and got into his Fairlane.

Externally, at least, he was merely a hard-nosed private detective who'd lost his leading client so he had to get out to hustle up some new business. Manhunting was what he did, and he was good at it.